Closure

Also by Terry Isaacson

A Flight Through Life

The Coronado Illusions

Closure

A Novel

Terry Isaacson

iUniverse, Inc.
New York   Bloomington

Closure

iUniverse books may be ordered through booksellers or by contacting:

iUniverse
1663 Liberty Drive
Bloomington, IN 47403
www.iuniverse.com
1-800-Authors (1-800-288-4677)

Because of the dynamic nature of the Internet, any Web addresses or links contained in this book may have changed since publication and may no longer be valid. The views expressed in this work are solely those of the author and do not necessarily reflect the views of the publisher, and the publisher hereby disclaims any responsibility for them.

ISBN: 978-1-4502-1899-3 (sc)
ISBN: 978-1-4502-2000-2 (dj)
ISBN: 978-1-4502-1900-6 (ebk)

Printed in the United States of America

iUniverse rev. date: 03/15/2010

Dedication

≋

To my family and *all* my friends—may we recognize and understand our differences—and work together to build a better world for generations to come.

Acknowledgments

~

Many people contributed generously to the development of characters and structure of the story for this novel.

My good friend, **Jerry Deland**, provided insight into life in Boulder during the 1970's as well as the corporate world of investment banking. **Charles Garcia, Dr. Ron Barnes, Sue Ross, Pamela Suarez** and **Vashti "Tice" Supplee** shared expertise in their professional areas. Long-time family friends **Betsy** and **Scott McLendon** highlighted scripture relevant to the story, as did my sister, **Janet Genung**.

Two fellow graduates of the US Air Force Academy helped develop realistic settings in two geographically separated, philosophically divergent cities. **David Samuel**, my Class of 1964 classmate and a retired Air Force colonel, assisted with research into residential neighborhoods, schools, hospitals and hotels in Boulder, and **Fletcher "Flash" Wiley**, Class of 1965 and one of the first African-American graduates of the Air Force Academy, helped me appreciate the complexity of culture and society in the greater Boston area.

Many residents were invaluable in helping me understand Boulder and the setting for my story. **Meg Sanders**, president of the Boulder High School football booster club, escorted me on my first visit to the school. **Bud Jenkins**, a 1971 BHS graduate and principal for the 2004-2008 school years, provided historical background on facilities and traditions at the high school. **Sue Zorichak**, the lead reunion planner for the BHS Class of 1977, described details and atmospherics of their class reunion and shared anecdotal experiences from their years in high school. Sue also convinced me to schedule the reunion in August and set the dinner dance at CU's Stadium Club, but unfortunately, that meant my characters had to be in the Class of 1978. Sorry, Sue, but you know it is really *your* class reunion on these pages. To **Sarah Huntley**, public information officer for the Boulder Police Department, and to **Barry and Sue Baer**, thanks for your time and attention to the details of my story.

And finally, to my lifetime companion **Nancy Isaacson**, for your insightful logic and instructive comments on the characters created for this fictional story, thanks for your love, understanding and support—again!

PROLOGUE

≈

J ack MacAdams regained consciousness when cold raindrops began pelting the exposed side of his face, the other cheek buried in a puddle of mud. Still stunned by a whack on the side of his head that caught him totally by surprise, he chose to remain frozen to the ground.

Slowly he cracked one eye open. A bright burst of lightning, followed immediately by a deafening roar of thunder, illuminated a nearby mountain ridge. Between the loud blasts of thunder, he listened for sounds around him. He heard only an angry wind whistling through the Colorado pines.

He waited a few more minutes. Then he struggled to his knees and touched his swollen head, just as another bolt of lightning pierced the black of the night. He looked with curiosity at the palm of his hand. He saw mud—and blood.

With every ounce of strength he could muster, MacAdams wobbled to his feet, stumbled forward a few steps and then dropped back to his knees, eventually settling his buttocks on the heels of his well-worn hiking boots.

He tried to clear his mind, to make sense of what had happened, but the pain emanating from his fractured skull dominated his thoughts. Though he wanted to move he was physically unable, and he slumped over on a bed of rocks and closed his eyes. Within seconds he had lost consciousness again.

The rain continued – a steady drizzle of tiny drops followed by a barrage of watery pellets pouring from an upset sky.

When MacAdams finally awoke, the rain had stopped and a half moon peeked through the thunderclouds dissipating over Eldorado Canyon. Still dazed, he rolled to his side, then, unsteadily, he struggled to his hands and knees.

Like a wounded prey waiting for another encounter with an attacker, he scanned the area with fearful eyes. A wispy column of smoke swirled from the campfire that had been extinguished first by campers and ultimately by the thunderstorm.

As he stared at the smoldering campfire, MacAdams' mind began to clear, and he recalled the events that led to the altercation.

It had been an exhilarating day in the canyon. His students had enjoyed the outing and their first experience at climbing a real mountain. He had formed the Mountain Climbing Club at Boulder High School and mentored them, encouraged them, taught them to hone their skills and enjoy the benefits of hiking, climbing and camping in his beloved Colorado. An expert technical climber, he had planned every detail of the day: transportation, trails, snacks and meals, water – yes, plenty of water – the cliffs to climb, and the campsite. The only unplanned activity was a midnight visit by one of his students and the unexpected arrival of a violent Rocky Mountain thunderstorm.

He shivered from the chilly air as he stood, the soft light of the moon barely illuminating the edge of a steep, craggy cliff. Carefully, he stepped forward and stared over the ledge, his arms and legs spread to steady his stance.

As quickly as it had ended, the thunderstorm erupted again, and a torrent of rain crashed down from the heavens above.

Then a furious display of lightning revealed the silhouette of the man still standing by the edge of the cliff—but when the next lightning bolt lashed out, he was gone.

CHAPTER ONE

~

L ance Carpenter stood at the window of his office on the thirty-seventh floor of the Prudential Tower in the Back Bay neighborhood of Boston. Mid-morning traffic still bustled around Copley Square while pedestrians casually strolled along the sidewalks with their shopping bags already filled.

About a mile to the west near a sweeping bend of the Charles River, he saw Fenway Park, and he savored the second Red Sox championship in the past four World Series. It had been eighty-six years between their triumphs in 1918 and 2004, but the Babe Ruth curse had finally been lifted, and Boston overflowed with believers and loyal Red Sox fans.

He turned from the window and paced deliberately around his office, surveying the collection of personal items and memorabilia. A gallery of photographs adorned one wall. Each picture had been neatly arranged around an acrylic painting of a fan-filled stadium in Tokyo, Japan. The scoreboard showed 0:00 time remaining, and the final score: Temple – 28; Boston College – 24. That game represented the low point in BC's storied football history, a winless 0-11 season, and the unfortunate, unceremonious end to Lance Carpenter's playing days—December 10, 1978.

From a library table centered below the painting, he picked up a silver-framed photograph of Kimberly and their two daughters taken during a summer visit to his wife's hometown of Camden, Maine. He smiled, placed it back on the table, and walked over to his massive executive desk with a single stack of papers arranged neatly in the center.

Lance picked up the top sheet, studied a colorful graphic for a few seconds, and tossed it back on the desk. With a deeply furrowed brow, he smoothed the slightly-graying hair along his temples with both hands. Then he turned to face the window and stared at the distant horizon that was pleasantly visible on this crisp, fall day. He did not hear the door open.

"Mr. Carpenter?"

Lance bristled, wheeled around and barked, "Arlene, I said no calls this morning."

"I know, sir, but there's someone who insists on talking with you now."

Except for slightly tousled hair and the displeasure of being interrupted clearly showing on his face, Lance Carpenter was a picture of perfection. At just over six feet tall and 185 pounds, he had maintained his playing weight during the years since his graduation from Boston College in 1982. His crisp white shirt was smooth from belt to collar, and the knot of his trademark maroon and gold tie fit snuggly around his athletic, seventeen-inch neck. From all outward appearances, Lance Carpenter looked as if he could still play football for the Eagles. Many alumni and long-time Boston College supporters were still disappointed that he never had that chance.

"All I need is fifteen minutes of quiet time before the board meeting. You know that."

"I'm sorry, Mr. Carpenter, but he says you'll want to talk with him."

"Well he's wrong, whoever *he* is. I don't want to talk with anyone now. Take a number and I'll return the call later today … maybe." Lance reached for the chart in the middle of the desk, studied it for a few seconds and then tossed it back onto the desk. He planted both hands on his hips to signal that the conversation was over.

"I already asked for his number, and he said he didn't want a return call. He said he wants to talk with you now. He said he's one of your high school classmates."

"For crying out loud, Arlene, am I supposed to drop everything and talk with someone I haven't spoken to for three decades? Who is this person who's screwing up my morning?"

Arlene glanced at her notepad and replied, "It's a Mr. Evans. Dexter Evans. He said you'd know him as Dee."

"Dee Evans?" he asked rhetorically, his eyes softening when he heard the familiar name from the past.

Lance Carpenter walked around the corner of his desk to within a few feet of his executive assistant, a matronly veteran administrator at Diversified Global Investment Bank who had been with him since his promotion to vice president two years ago. He spoke quietly, the irritation and tension in his voice replaced by a calm, confident tone. "Is my presentation all set in the board room, Arlene?"

"Yes, sir, eighteen slides. They're all ready to go. I checked them myself a few minutes ago."

Lance reached out and gently wrapped his arm around her shoulder. "Thanks, Arlene. I know I can always count on you." Together they walked to the door, and with a final pat on the back, he continued, "Mr. Evans and I were best friends in high school. You can tell him I'd be pleased to speak with him for a few minutes."

Arlene smiled and turned to leave, closing the door behind her.

Lance raised the cuff of his shirt and noted the time on his wristwatch. He briskly returned to his desk and sat down. With less than ten minutes to the start of the most important board meeting of his professional career, Lance Carpenter stared at the telephone and waited for Arlene to transfer the call from a high school buddy he had not seen for more than thirty years. "Lance Carpenter," he said after one ring.

"You sure run a tight front office, Mr. Carpenter."

"Well I'll be damned. A voice from the distant past, and I could recognize it anywhere, anytime. It's good to hear from you, Dee. How long's it been?"

"The last time I saw you was during the summer of 1978, the day you left Boulder for Boston. By the way, Arlene was very nice. I badgered her but she stayed calm, very professional. You've got a winner there."

"You got that right. She knows the ropes around here. Keeps me squared away, and that's tough to do these days."

Dexter Eugene Evans propped his well-worn loafers on the coffee table that sat in front of a crumpled sofa and his comfortable leather chair. An empty coffee cup rested on yesterday's edition of the *San Jose Times*. Wearing loose fitting jeans and a long-sleeved polo shirt, he settled his head against the back of the chair and closed his eyes while he spoke. "My sources tell me things are going very well for you on the East Coast. You must like New England."

"So far, so good. There are no mountains out here, but life's been good to me. Are you still in Palo Alto?"

"No more. I moved my business to San Jose in 1991. We still have the home in Boulder." Dee leaned forward and plopped an elbow on his knee while continuing to talk on the cell phone. "My sources tell me you married a gal from New England."

"You must have a lot of sources."

"Is that true? You married?"

Lance stood up and said, "Yes, that's true. I've been married for twenty-four years now. We have two daughters—one is twenty-one and the other eighteen. But you know, Dee, I've got a board meeting in a few minutes, so I have to …"

"You have to what? You have to hang up on your old buddy? Don't you even want to know why I called out of the blue?"

"Of course I do, but I really have to get moving to the board room. They always start precisely on time and I don't want to be late. Can I call you back later today?"

"Oh, you'll be okay. Just walk in and tell them you've been talking with a friend from high school you haven't heard from in thirty years. I'm sure they'll understand."

"To be honest, Dee, there's a lot riding on this board meeting.

There are only two major agenda items, and I'm making one of the presentations. If it goes well ..."

"If it goes well, you'll be promoted to managing director," Dee interrupted.

"I want to know who your sources are," he said, shaking his head in disbelief.

"I can't tell you that, but I can tell you why I'm calling today."

Lance reached for the colored chart in the middle of his desk and reviewed it one last time while he impatiently listened to what Dee Evans had to say.

"It's about our thirty-year class reunion, Lance. You haven't been back to Boulder for years, and this reunion should be a good time. Rebecca Carlin has been reaching out to all our classmates and she asked me to give you a call. She said you haven't responded to her email."

"Rebecca Carlin? I don't remember getting any email from her. Maybe it was screened as junk mail."

"Maybe you saw her name and hit delete. As I recall, the two of you weren't on the best of terms when you left Boulder."

"That's putting it nicely, Dee. We weren't even speaking to each other and it got pretty ugly." Lance lowered the chart to his side and slowly turned back to the window, his mind preoccupied with his presentation for the board of directors. "When's the reunion?"

"It's in August."

"I'll have to give it some thought. To tell you the truth, I haven't had much interest in returning to Boulder."

Dee sensed Lance's uncertainty. "While you're thinking about it, let me give you another reason to come back for our thirtieth reunion. I just found out the high school selected me as the Distinguished Citizen of the Year for 2008. Can you imagine that—Dexter Evans a distinguished anything? It would mean a lot to me if Lance Carpenter were there to share the honor. Whether you believe it or not, it would never have been possible without your friendship."

"Wow, distinguished citizen? That's great news, Dee. Congratulations!"

"Thanks, my friend. I hope you'll give some serious thought to coming back for the reunion. And remember, if you're late to the board meeting, just walk in there with full confidence, make your presentation, and be ready for all the predictable questions. Tompkins is on your side."

When the call concluded, Lance straightened his BC tie, slipped on his suit coat and headed for the board room.

As he entered the meeting already in progress, Lance wondered, *How in the hell does Dee know Paul Tompkins?*

CHAPTER TWO

~

The quarterly board of directors meeting of the financial conglomerate Diversified Global Investment Bank had begun precisely at 10:00 a.m. Eastern Standard Time. The regional corporate offices in Chicago, Denver and San Francisco had been connected by video conferencing technology seven minutes prior to the scheduled start time. Some members of the board were seated at their designated places at a huge conference table, and others were engaged in various conversations when the Chairman of the Board, J. Paul Tompkins, called the meeting to order with two taps of a solid mahogany gavel.

At the head of the table, Chairman Tompkins projected an image of authority—dark gray suit, white shirt with deep maroon tie, silver cufflinks visible when he raised an arm to remove his reading glasses. The years had begun to show age on his pleasantly rounded face, but the color of his hair and neatly-trimmed moustache left no doubt. With a goatee, many people thought he would be a spitting image of Colonel Sanders.

Tompkins sat facing an array of four video screens mounted high on the wall so that everyone in the room would have an unobstructed view of each screen. He spoke with the presiding officer at each of the satellite locations and then, for the benefit of first-time attendees, asked each member of the board of directors for a brief, personal introduction.

When they finished their comments, a title slide for the first agenda item appeared on the Boston screen. Tompkins scanned the room looking for the person he had tasked to present the corporation's annual budget with projections for each operating division.

"It looks as if we have a notable absentee this morning. Let's go to the next topic on the agenda, and can someone find out what's happened to Mr. Carpenter?"

A young man in the back of the board room leapt up and headed for the door. A board member glared at the chairman, closed the binder in front of her and sat back in her chair with an audible sigh. Another woman walked to the far end of the room to address the board.

As she began an update on national trends in the housing and credit sectors and the impact on projected fourth quarter unemployment, Lance slipped quietly into the room and sat down at the only empty seat at the table, the one nearest the presentation podium. The woman stopped talking momentarily while Lance pulled his chair forward and offered an apologetic glance, which she ignored. Others shifted in their seats during the awkward, unexpected diversion from the board meeting's tightly-scripted agenda.

"Go on," Tompkins ordered. "There should be no more distractions." He looked at Lance Carpenter while he spoke, and most people in the room read the chairman's comment as a rebuke for his tardiness. After all, he was responsible for the featured topic at the most important board meeting of his life—and he had just arrived five minutes late.

The speaker at the podium, Marcella Rhodes, nodded to the chairman and resumed talking about the very real possibility of unemployment in the country reaching five percent, which would be the highest level in the last two years and would be certain to shake Wall Street and the credit markets.

Marcella Rhodes certainly knew her stuff. She had been recruited by a reputable investment banking firm in New York City after completing her baccalaureate and master's programs at Harvard in less than five years, start to finish. Since coming to Diversified Global Investment

Bank seven years ago, she had impressed senior management and rocketed to the vice president position well ahead of her contemporaries. Though no one ever talked about it openly, everyone in the Boston office assumed Marcella Rhodes and Lance Carpenter were on a collision course for the next available managing director position.

Marcella was not only intellectually brilliant, but she was also a very attractive woman. With her complete package of beauty, poise and professional expertise, she had garnered significant respect in the financial industry and built the reputation of a woman with potential to reach the top of a major corporation. That is, if her cold-blooded ambition didn't sidetrack her along the way.

When Marcella finished her presentation, she stepped away from the podium and stood at the far end of the table. "Mr. Chairman, members of the board," she said coolly as she smoothed the front of her tailored navy suit, "I'd be happy to respond to any questions you may have."

"Any questions for Ms. Rhodes?" Paul Tompkins let the question hang while he scanned the room for inquiries and reaction to her presentation. Detecting none, he said, "I have one, Marcella. What do you think your friends at the Fed will do if unemployment hits five percent?"

She smiled and spoke confidently. "Of course that's a hypothetical, sir, but we all know the facts. The subprime mortgage crisis is real. People all over the country are feeling the stress of increased debt. Merrill Lynch just took a $7.9 billion write down for subprime mortgages and asset-backed bonds. O'Neill is history. He led Merrill to its biggest loss in ninety-three years. Countrywide is in trouble, too. They posted a $1.2 billion loss in the third quarter, their first quarterly loss in twenty-five years, and I'm hearing Bank of America is pitching an offer to purchase Countrywide in the magnitude of $4 to 5 billion before the end of the year. People whisper the term 'R-word' as if actually saying 'recession' will trigger the inevitable. Remember, 2008 is an election year—and with economic indicators trending the way they are—if I were queen for a day at the Fed, I'd cut the prime by a quarter in a New York second! That's what I think, sir."

"You've never been afraid to state your case, Marcella. And if I were king for a day at the Fed, I'd cut the key to three point five right now, and then another half at the meeting next week," he said watching for reaction from around the room.

No one dared counter the chairman in this setting.

"Any more questions for Ms. Rhodes?" Tompkins continued to scan the room for additional questions, and seeing none, he said, "Thank you, Marcella." Then, without looking directly at him, he asked dryly, "Are you ready for your presentation, Mr. Carpenter? Or do you need more time?"

Lance slid his chair back, stood up and began talking as he walked a few feet to the podium. "Yes, sir, Mr. Chairman, members of the board, I'm ready. I apologize for being late this morning."

Tompkins grimaced and asked indignantly, "What? Were you giving Coach Jag suggestions on the game plan for Florida State tomorrow? I see you're wearing your trademark BC tie again."

"Only on Fridays and at fundraisers, Mr. Chairman." Lance looked down at the diagonal maroon and gold stripes on his necktie, and with two fingers of his right hand he gently waved it for show.

Marcella scowled at the exchange; however, neither Lance nor J. Paul Tompkins noticed, nor would they have cared.

"I got a call from a high school classmate right before the meeting. Someone I haven't heard from for more than thirty years," Lance said as he pressed a button on the remote calling for the first slide of his presentation. "We talked longer than I expected, and I'm sorry for being late. I'm ready when you are, sir."

Chairman Tompkins did not speak. He simply sat back in his seat and with a single nod of his head gave Lance the green light to begin.

"This corporation faces the most difficult challenge of its thirty five-year history," Lance began. He spoke deliberately and with brimming confidence, just like Dee Evans had suggested. By the time he flashed the second chart on the screen, he had the full attention of everyone in the Boston meeting as well as those watching in Chicago, Denver and

San Francisco. Even Marcella Rhodes paid attention to every word he spoke.

For the next fifteen minutes, Lance delivered his message with authority. Diversified Global Investment Bank had lost market share to competitors in each of the last five years. A sequence of major organizational changes and too-rapid diversification had weakened the balance sheet. Lance's proposed operating budget for 2008 included significant cost cutting measures with an emphasis on short term financial results, including closing one of the three regional offices, a recommendation that raised eyebrows and elevated blood pressure for many of the people listening to his report.

"Any questions?" Lance asked as he blackened the screen and casually stepped to the side of the podium, waiting for someone to speak.

Tompkins surveyed the room and a director near the end of the table spoke up. "Mr. Carpenter, close a regional office? In your considered judgment, what is the root cause for the economic trends we're seeing today?"

"I'll give you my personal opinion, sir. The problem began with the Community Restoration Act and the requirement for banks to underwrite ten percent of their mortgages for low income, first time home buyers. Add to that all the people who think they can afford a $400,000 mortgage making seventy-five grand a year, and you've got millions in high risk notes on the books. It's going to come back and bite us one of these days."

"Any other questions?" asked the chairman with a hint of finality.

When no one spoke up, Lance closed his briefing folder and returned to his seat without further comment. His heart was pounding but his outward demeanor suggested total commitment to his message and complete self-confidence. *Thank you Dee Evans*, he thought to himself.

With the two major presentations completed, Tompkins ticked through the remaining items on the agenda, and with little or no discussion on each, he concluded the meeting ten minutes ahead of the printed termination time.

Terry Isaacson

Body language and facial expressions reflected an uncharacteristic tension for a Diversified Global Investment Bank board meeting. Lance and the board member to his left had leaned forward with both elbows on the table and were talking shoulder-to-shoulder when Paul Tompkins approached from behind. Placing his hand on Lance's back, he said, "I'd like to see you in my office."

"Of course. Now or ..."

Tompkins turned and walked away before Lance finished.

"You better go now. He didn't look happy," the board member said. "Matter of fact, I'm not very happy either. You dealt the board—and the chairman—a low blow."

Lance stood and said, "These are tough times, and things will get worse before they get better. You can count on it."

He grabbed his portfolio and headed straight to the chairman's office.

CHAPTER THREE

~

Lance's mind whirled as he bounded up the stairwell to the thirty-ninth floor. *I blew it. Never should have taken Dee's call,* he thought. He reached the top of the stairs and flashed an encoded card past a security sensor. When he heard the lock buzz, he pulled the heavy metal door open. At the end of a long corridor, an array of floor-to-ceiling glass panels marked the entrance to the chairman's suite where J. Paul Tompkins would be waiting.

Word had spread quickly after the board meeting, and everyone in the chairman's office knew that Carpenter had been summoned by JP, the moniker given to the founder of Diversified Global Investment Bank nearly thirty-five years ago.

Lance stopped at the door. He took a couple of deep breaths to release the tension in his chest. *Okay, here we go.*

No one spoke to Lance when he entered the outer office. JP's office director simply turned her eyes toward the chairman's door, as if to say, *He's waiting.* They exchanged strained smiles, and when Lance passed by she mouthed, "*Good luck.*"

JP had been sitting on the front edge of his desk and he immediately leapt to his feet when Lance came into the room. "Close one of the regional offices?" he hissed. "Where in the hell did that come from?" His words paced through clenched teeth; his cheeks were puffed and reddened.

Lance stopped and stood in the middle of the chairman's office. From the flush on JP's face, he knew it was still not time to answer.

By now the two men were only a few feet apart, Lance standing ramrod straight, still looking sharp in his pinstriped navy blue suit and colorful BC tie. Clearly agitated, JP started to turn away and then abruptly squared off in front of the young man, his eyes flashing fire. "And why didn't you clear that with me?" he thundered. "I should fire you on the spot!"

Lance flinched instinctively when he heard the words, but he gathered himself before responding. "It was a last minute thought, sir. It was actually triggered by the phone call, and I apologize for raising the topic at the board meeting. In retrospect, bad idea."

"*Very* bad idea, young man. It could cost you your career. Sit down over there." JP pointed to an arrangement of four chairs, one on each side of a small square table with a pitcher of ice water and four glasses in the middle. Having relieved some of his emotion with the initial tirade, JP slid his fingers through a head full of wavy, white hair, still one of the distinguishing physical characteristics of his persona. He walked back to his desk and sat down. After a long silence, he pulled a pen from the center drawer, hastily scrawled something on a notepad and ripped off the top sheet of paper.

Lance waited … worried.

JP pressed a button on his telephone console, and the office director appeared within a few seconds. As she approached the desk he leaned forward, holding at arm's length the note he had written. "Ten minutes," JP said. She took the paper without hesitation and read the note as she left the room.

While Lance sat alone anticipating the next shoe to drop, he pondered the situation he was in. He had known J. Paul Tompkins for almost three decades, and he'd never seen him so furious. And now, as the single focal point of the chairman's anger, Lance felt a dull ache in the pit of his stomach, a sensation that intensified when JP sat down in the chair facing him.

"Mr. Carpenter," the chairman began with ominous formality, "do you have any idea why I'm so disappointed in the stunt you pulled today?"

Lance cleared his throat and said, "I'm sorry about being late, sir. It will never happen again."

Tompkins gently shook his head. He settled back in the chair with his forearms resting naturally on the sides, both feet planted on the floor. "You know, Lance, I'm seventy-two years old. I started this company thirty-five years ago. I'm going to step aside in the next year or two and give someone the opportunity of a lifetime." He looked directly into Lance's dark blue eyes as he spoke.

Lance had been in the chairman's office many times, but this was the first time he had been summoned for a good old-fashioned ass chewing. He listened intently to every word.

"Do you have any idea who I want to replace me?" JP leaned forward and folded his hands in his lap. "Don't answer that. I'll tell you," he added quickly as he sprang to his feet waving an index finger a few inches from Lance's face. He circled behind his chair and the hand with the waving finger turned to a clenched fist.

"Yoouuu," he snarled, the word hanging until he slammed his fist down on top of the chair. "You, Lance Carpenter, are the person I want to take over the reins of this company."

JP straightened and dropped his arms to his sides, the tension and anger subsiding rapidly with his revelation. "Until today," he continued, his voice softening with a hint of regret. "Now I'm not so sure."

Lance said nothing. He looked down at the floor. *Have I been fired?* The question flashed in his mind as he waited to hear what more the chairman had to say.

"Lance, you're a great young man with terrific potential." J. Paul Tompkins had gathered his emotions and sounded like a father encouraging his son after a major disappointment in life. "I've worked you into all the key management positions, and you've worked hard and produced great results. People like you, they respect you, you've got leadership charisma—and you've got the smarts to go along with it."

"Thank you, sir, I want to ..."

"Let me finish," the chairman said quietly.

Lance braced for the worst.

"You threw a hunk of raw meat on the table today—without my prior approval. You know better than that." JP paused and reached for the pitcher of ice water. He filled the nearest glass and offered it to Lance, who declined with a shake of the head. "You and Marcella were in the spotlight for a reason," JP continued. "I wanted the board to see you in action. And you show up late and throw me a curve ball. What the hell were you thinking?"

Lance had been mulling over thoughts as he listened to the chairman's message. "I apologize again for being late, sir, and I regret the recommendation to close a regional office without giving you a heads up. But I stand by everything I said today, and if that gets me fired, then so be it."

"Fired? Don't give me anything more to think about."

"Maybe I should reach for silence."

"No, Lance, that's not the answer. But I've got another question for you."

Lance detected a trace of twinkle in the chairman's eyes, and he began to feel a bit more secure. "And that is?"

"What regional office should we close?"

"Denver."

"Why Denver?"

Lance was prepared for this question. "Chicago's solid. They're ahead of every projection. San Francisco's got some challenges, but they've got a good team in place and the trends are all positive. Denver's a disaster. They're way behind on earnings and we're looking at losses in the magnitude of twenty-eight to thirty-two percent for the quarter. Christine's in way over her head as the regional VP."

"The board loves her."

"The board loves women VPs."

"I'll be damned. I never thought I'd hear you say anything negative about a colleague. Are you trying to save your own ass?"

"No, sir. You asked me what office to close and why—and I told you what I thought."

J. Paul Tompkins sat back and smiled for the first time since the board meeting ended. "Let me tell you what I think, Lance. I think you're right on target. You must've read my mind. I've been thinking about replacing Christine out there in Denver for quite some time." He glanced at his wristwatch, and this time he stood up slowly, nodding his head in agreement with his own thought. "Since you brought it up at the board meeting today, here's what I want you to do."

Sensing the end of the discussion, Lance also stood and waited for the chairman's charge.

"I want you to come up with a plan for downsizing Denver over the next nine months. We can replace Christine and make whatever organizational changes you think are necessary."

"The rating agencies will have a field day with that one, sir."

"I don't care what the rating agencies think. They don't run this company, I do!"

A double buzz on the intercom interrupted the conversation. JP again checked the time and then continued speaking as he and Lance walked toward the office door.

"There's one more thing I want you to think about." JP turned the knob, and with the door still closed, he said, "I want you to think about taking over the Denver office."

He opened the door, stared directly into Lance's eyes and said, "And I'd like your answer by Monday morning."

Then JP Tompkins patted Lance on the back, the signal for him to depart.

The folks in the chairman's outer office saw the glazed look on Lance's face as he walked past without speaking.

Lance Carpenter had no idea whether he had just been fired or promoted. He only knew he had a lot to talk about when he got home.

CHAPTER FOUR

~

T he Carpenter's home in Andover, an upscale suburb about thirty-five minutes from downtown Boston, looked unpretentious from the narrow, tree-lined street that wound to the top of Chelsea Hill. Even long-time residents called the drive to Boston "chaotic" in good weather. In snow or rain it was treacherous.

They had lived in Andover for twenty years, raised two daughters who had graduated from a nearby private school and decided to follow their mother's footsteps at Boston University. Three years apart, the older daughter, now a junior, had been the first to live on the BU Charles River Campus, and her younger sister had moved into an historic brownstone residence hall on Bay State Road in August.

That gave Kimberly Carpenter the opportunity to refocus on her own career, which she had decided to put on hold until the kids were in college. She felt a void in her life when her daughters left home, but with Lance doing well at work and several offers on the table for her consideration, she believed their future held great promise.

Kimberly was anxious to see Lance when he got home. She had good news to share. She had spent the morning doing volunteer work on behalf of the Essex County district attorney's office, and that afternoon she had pampered herself with a spa day—manicure, pedicure, hair colored and styled. There was a bounce in her step as she prepared a plate of thin turkey slices and wheat crackers, and slices of Swiss cheese artfully carved into one-inch squares. From the wine rack in the family room, she pulled a bottle of Kendall Jackson chardonnay – Lance's favorite – and nestled the bottle into a silver bucket filled with ice. She placed the snack plate and two wine glasses on the coffee table, popping a single piece of cheese into her mouth before she covered the goodies with a paper towel.

After fiddling with the components in Lance's entertainment center for a few minutes, Norah Jones appeared on the high definition screen. She sat at a shiny black grand piano singing "Be Here To Love Me," her soft, mellow voice filling the air:

> *Who cares what the night watchmen say,*
> *The stage has been set for the play,*
> *Just hold me and tell me,*
> *You'll be here to love me today.*

Kimberly drifted along a wall of built-in shelves in the family room where framed photos rekindled memories of her first years together with Lance.

They had met in January of 1979 while Lance recuperated from knee surgery resulting from a grotesque injury during the Boston College/ Temple football game played in Tokyo, Japan four weeks earlier. As a heavily recruited quarterback from Boulder, Colorado, freshman Lance Carpenter had engineered a fourth quarter drive for what could have been the winning touchdown, when his right leg planted on the turf and 800 pounds of Temple tacklers twisted him to the ground. Still on crutches and undergoing daily physical therapy, Lance spent the afternoons at the offices of a technology research and publishing firm owned by an entrepreneurial BC alumnus.

He'd been there only a week when he saw a perky, petite young lady emerge from the general counsel's office carrying an armload of thick files. She wore a knee-length skirt that swooshed from side to side as she walked. Her auburn hair was tied in a ponytail in back, and it, too, waved with each step. Kimberly Keck noticed the guy on crutches, smiled and trekked off down the hall.

That same day as they both were leaving the building, they met by chance on the elevator. Lance later wondered whether Kimberly had planned it that way. By the time they reached the ground floor, they had learned enough to maintain interest in each other.

Kimberly had graduated from Newport College and was trying to get into law school at Harvard or Boston University, working while studying for the LSAT. Lance had played football at BC and was hoping to play again the following fall. They were both going to be working on the same floor for the next several months, so they parted with a wave and a smile.

From then on, not a day went by that Lance Carpenter and Kimberly Keck did not find time for each other.

By summertime Lance could walk. But rehabilitation was slow, and although therapy continued, it became doubtful that he'd be ready to play football by the fall of 1980.

On her first taking of the LSAT, Kimberly scored in the ninety-sixth percentile and waited for acceptance to law school—any of the ten law schools she had applied to. Within a two week period she received seven rejection letters, including one from Harvard University where she had set her heart. So when the Boston University School of Law approved her application, she readily accepted and began planning for entry in August 1980.

Theirs had been a storybook romance from the beginning. He, the star athlete whose playing career had tragically ended, and she, the attractive young woman determined to be successful in the field of criminal justice. It was a profession dominated by men, but a dean at Newport College who had become a professor after a distinguished career in the Federal Bureau of Investigation, encouraged women to enter it.

When it was certain that he could never play competitively again, Lance turned to the world of corporate finance and took advantage of opportunities offered by a sympathetic BC graduate, a turning point that proved beneficial for Lance and the graduate's company. Kimberly started law school at BU pursuing a *Juris Doctorate* degree with a concentration in finance law.

With their individual professional goals and objectives aligned, Lance Carpenter and Kimberly Keck decided to get married, and in the summer of 1981 they were pronounced man and wife at the altar of Our Lady of Good Hope Catholic Church in Camden, Maine, about a mile from Kimberly's home on Chestnut Hill.

Kimberly beamed at a photo of the bride and groom at their reception in Laite Beach Memorial Park, their backs to picturesque Camden Bay in the background. It was the beginning of their life together, and with every year it had gotten better and better. She was holding the photo in her hands and swaying to the soothing sounds of Norah Jones when Lance came in and tossed his briefcase on the chair.

The noise startled her and abruptly ended her daydreaming of years-gone-by. She returned the wedding photo to its rightful place, and turning to Lance she said, "Hello, dear, how was your day?"

"Very interesting. How 'bout yours?"

"Well, you tell me." Kimberly stood a few feet away, holding her hands in front of her with fingers spread, all ten perfectly polished nails proudly on display.

"Very nice, my dear," Lance said, admiring her delicate hands and freshly manicured nails. "And let's see, you're wearing black slacks with a teal vest over a long sleeved white blouse? You look just like a fashion model right off the pages of *Vogue*."

"Well, thank you. The slacks are new, too."

Lance nodded his approval and said, "Hey, you shortened your hair! Let me see the back."

Kimberly turned her head first one way and then the other, touching her new "do" with the tips of her fingers as she spoke. "I had it bobbed. We took off two to three inches. You like it?"

"Yeah. It looks great," he replied with a smile.

Lance then noticed the empty wine glasses and a plate of snacks on the coffee table. He saw the bottle of wine in the silver bucket. "I'll open that bottle," he said, the tone in his voice dimming. Kimberly thought she detected a hint of gloom when he said, "We need to talk."

Lance uncorked the bottle of KJ chardonnay and filled their glasses. Kimberly removed the napkin from the cheese and crackers and rolled up a slice of turkey.

They settled in their chairs and began sharing the events of their respective days. Within a few minutes, Kimberly knew her initial perception was accurate. Not only was Lance's recount of the day gloomy, it was downright scary.

CHAPTER FIVE

~

"There's no way we're moving to Denver," Kimberly bellowed. "He just asked me to think about it, Kim. It's not a done deal, but he wants an answer by Monday."

"You can think about it all you want. We're not leaving Boston. Not now. Not with two daughters at BU. Not with you about to be promoted and me ready to resume my own career."

Kimberly drained her glass of wine and set the glass down. She picked up the empty plate and held it on her lap. "It's out of the question."

Lance reached for the bottle and offered to refill her glass, and when she declined, he filled his own. "I don't think you understand, Kim. I may have no other options after today. JP told me I was his choice to replace him as CEO, which is hard to believe. Why would he tell me that now? That's a year or two away and by no means a certainty. Especially after today. But I have to at least *think* about taking over the Denver office."

Kimberly grabbed her empty glass and slid to the front edge of her seat. "I'll give you something else to think about. I love you very much, but if you go to Denver, you'll go alone. I'm not leaving Boston. Not now. Not ever."

"Oh, for Christ's sake, Kim. I don't need your ultimatum. I need your understanding. I don't want to leave New England, and I'd never move without you. You know that."

Kimberly stood, and with an apologetic smile she said, "I know, dear. But you've been so caught up in this Denver thing that I don't think you heard me. I'm going back to work full time."

"You're what?"

"You know I've talked about going back to work when both girls are in college."

"Kimberly Carpenter, you haven't worked full time since Andrea was born. You really think you're ready for that?" Lance grabbed the knot on his maroon and gold tie, and in one full motion pulled it from his neck and tossed it on the coffee table. He unbuttoned the top button of his shirt, sat back and waited for a response.

Kimberly walked slowly toward the kitchen, thinking about a more delicate way to make her case. For twenty-six years she had lived with Lance's highs and lows, his successes and disappointments, and she loved him dearly. He had been a wonderful husband and father and had built a rewarding career in the financial industry as he steadily moved up the corporate ladder. Yet whenever he faced conflict or major challenges in his life, Lance internalized his feelings and buried his thoughts. She thought her initial reaction to the possibility of moving to Denver may have upset him, and she was right.

When she returned to the family room, Kimberly sat down on the arm of Lance's chair, wrapped both of her arms around him and squeezed affectionately.

Lance sat stiffly, but kissed her on the nape of the neck.

"I think I know what you're going through, dear," she said softly, her arms still holding him gently. "You've been preparing for today for months. You know Tompkins likes you and you'll do whatever he says. And now, he's asked you to do something you know you can't do—and that's got you torn apart."

Lance kissed her again as she released the hug and sat up, her emerald eyes scanning the features of his face. He looked worn and weary after a tough week at work and the events of the day.

"Perhaps we need a little down time, Lance," she said, her fingers lightly moving along his temple to the back of his head. "Maybe we need a little together time."

Lance sipped his wine while he listened, still buried deep in thought.

"I'm feeling a bit lonely these days. With both of the girls gone, and you at work twelve hours a day, I have a lot of time to think. And yes, I think I'm ready to go back to work full time."

Lance had waited for the answer, but still he did not speak.

Sensing his withdrawal, Kimberly moved back to her own seat. "All you've thought about for the past few months is your work and your big board meeting." Her eyes twinkled when they finally made contact with his, and she continued, "… and Boston College football!"

"They're undefeated, Kim. Eight wins and no losses. Ranked number two in the country."

"Who do they play tomorrow?"

"Florida State."

For the first time since he had come home, Kimberly saw a sparkle in his eyes. "Are we going?" she asked innocently, knowing full well the answer.

"Are you playing with me?"

"I'd like to—if we can ever find time."

Lance laughed, his pearly whites flashing when he said, "There you go again, sweetheart, trying to take advantage of me when I'm vulnerable. I suppose you'd like me to open another bottle of wine."

"I've already done that. It's in the refrigerator."

"I'll get it," Lance said as he picked up his tie and draped it around his neck. "What's for dinner?"

"I'm going to warm up the lasagna."

"Good. I love your lasagna," he said as he disappeared into the kitchen.

Lance returned with the chardonnay and promptly filled both glasses. "If we win tomorrow and LSU gets beat, we could be number one in the country. What do you think about that, Kim?"

"Gee, that would be good, wouldn't it?" she asked coquettishly.

Lance smirked and filled his mouth with wine.

"Did your friend get in touch with you today?"

"Dee Evans? Yeah, he called right before the board meeting."

"He said his name was Dexter."

"You talked to him?"

"Yes, he called here this morning and we actually had quite a pleasant conversation. He seemed like a nice guy and it sounded as if you were good friends in high school."

"We were—but we were as different as night and day. He sure picked a bad time to call. Made me late for the board meeting." Lance shook his head as he thought about walking in right in the middle of Marcella's presentation, and he recalled Dee's words: *Just walk in there with full confidence … Tompkins is on your side.*

Surprised, Kimberly said, "You're never late. How'd you let that happen?"

"I don't know, Kim. We just kept talking and I couldn't break it off. I was five minutes late and JP was not a happy camper."

"Ohhhh," she murmured, the full impact of Lance's day finally sinking in.

"Dee wants me to go back to our thirtieth class reunion. He's getting some award, and from what I've learned, he really deserves it. He started his own software development firm and it's probably making two or three hundred million a year. Not bad for the guy most people thought was the number one nerd in our class."

Kimberly sipped her wine. "He said I'd like Colorado. Said Boulder's an interesting place, and August is a great time for a reunion. I told him I've never been west of the Mississippi."

"I'm not going back to any high school reunion, Kim. It won't matter if I *never* go back to Boulder!" Lance plopped his empty glass back on the coffee table and pushed back in his chair. "I have no interest in returning to Colorado—not even if it means the end of my career."

Lance's emphatic reaction to the possibility of returning to Colorado for a high school reunion surprised her. Over the years, Kimberly Carpenter had seen her husband go up and down like a yo-yo, and she knew he was on his way back down.

"What time's the game tomorrow?" she asked, hoping to lure Lance back to one of his favorite topics.

"It's a night game and it's going to be cold and rainy."

"Won't matter, we'll be inside, won't we?"

"Always, my dear."

"Great," she said as she stood up and started to the kitchen. "You ready for some lasagna?"

"Sure am," he answered, watching her walk away. "Hey!" he called to her. "I *really* like your hair."

CHAPTER SIX

≈

O vercast skies and a cold, blustery rain dominated the Boston area as Lance drove to work on Monday morning – just what he needed after a misery-filled weekend.

On Saturday night the Eagles had lost to Florida State, 27-17. Lance and Kimberly sat with a group of donors in the comfort of a suite in Alumni Stadium while every football nut in the country watched the game on national television. At kickoff, the remnants of Hurricane Noel dumped buckets of frigid rain on the field, and fifty-mile per hour winds whipped the flags and pennants and made 40,000 loyal fans downright miserable.

Lance was uncharacteristically quiet during the game. Kimberly thought she knew why, so she too sat quietly and let Lance concentrate on the play of the Eagles and their star quarterback, Heisman candidate Matt Ryan. Trailing the entire game, Ryan threw two touchdown passes in the second half to close the gap to three points: 20-17. Then with about a minute remaining, Ryan's pass was intercepted and returned for a touchdown—and the Boston College Eagles, ranked number two in the country, were knocked from the ranks of the unbeaten.

The last minute interception triggered a deep seated memory in Lance Carpenter's mind. Thirty years ago on a windy, chilly night in Mile High Stadium, Boulder High School played in the Colorado AAA State Championship playoffs. He – Boulder High's star quarterback

– had thrown three interceptions, including one that was returned for a touchdown in the final minute of play. It was the worst – and last – performance of Lance's high school career, and his team had lost 27-17.

As Lance sat dumbstruck in the suite, it was as if a legion of inner demons had been awakened. Kimberly tried to reach him by reminding him that it was just a game, but she was unsuccessful. Lance uttered only a few words during the drive home.

His funk continued on Sunday, and twice during the day he brought up the topic of moving to Denver. Each time Kimberly told him he would have to go alone.

* * *

On Monday morning, Lance turned south onto Massachusetts Highway 28, the heavy rain slowing traffic to a crawl.

At least he had an additional hour to make up his mind about a trip to Colorado. It was a decision that could very well cost him his job.

Except for giving him more time to think, the long commute did nothing positive for Lance's state of mind. He parked, hustled through the lobby to the elevator and punched number thirty-seven on the panel of floor selections. With everyone still wearing their raincoats and holding soaked umbrellas, the air in the enclosed elevator felt heavy with humidity.

One of the passengers recognized Lance Carpenter and spoke to him. "Tough loss last night," he said. "I thought we were going to see another Virginia Tech."

Ordinarily Lance would have more to say about the game, but he simply muttered, "Yeah, tough loss." The door opened at the thirty-seventh floor, and without any further conversation, Lance stepped out and headed for his office.

"Good morning, Mr. Carpenter."

"Morning, Arlene." He managed a smile for his office director.

"Don't say anything about the game," he cautioned, waving a black leather glove in the air. "You can let Mr. Tompkins know I'm here. He asked to see me first thing this morning."

"He's not in yet, sir."

"Okay, then let me know when he calls."

"Yes, sir, I will."

"Is the coffee ready?"

"A fresh pot's brewing. We've already finished the first one."

"Thank you, Arlene. Holler when it's ready," he said as he closed the door behind him.

Lance had taken only a couple of sips of the hot coffee when Arlene called to say J. Paul Tompkins was ready to see him. He took another drink and set the cup down on a coaster on a credenza by the window. The rain had stopped for the moment, but from the looks of the dark, dreary clouds, Lance knew the storm was far from over.

This time Lance climbed the stairs slowly to the thirty-ninth floor. At the top of the staircase, he waved his ID at the sensor and pulled the door open when it buzzed. He strolled down the hallway to the chairman's suite and walked straight to Tompkins' office.

The chairman met him at the door and extended his arm for a handshake. "Good morning, Lance," he said as if the sun was shining and all was well with the world.

Lance gripped his hand and squeezed, a firm handshake being one of his personal trademarks.

"Three interceptions. Three!" Tompkins shook his head. "But they almost pulled it out again."

"I knew the Seminoles would come in here ready to play. They're probably the best team in the country with three losses."

"That'll hurt Ryan's chances for the Heisman. Three interceptions in a big game on national TV? Not a good night." Chairman Tompkins pointed to a chair for Lance to sit. It was not the same one he had taken last Friday night.

"It was a miserable night. A few bright spots, but a tough loss,"

Lance said as he sat down. "Matt'll be back though. He's a great competitor."

"I think you're right. He'll bounce back," Tompkins said, settling into his wing-backed leather chair. "Enough of that, Lance. Let's talk about Colorado. Have you given that some thought?"

"Yes, sir. All weekend."

"Did you and Kimberly talk about a move?"

"Yes, sir. All weekend."

"And?"

Lance looked directly into the chairman's eyes and said boldly, "If I move to Colorado, I'm going alone."

"That's not good."

"I know."

"That presents a problem," JP said. "I've got to make some changes in Denver, and I think you're the right man for the job. You can consider it a promotion. Let's say it's the final stepping stone before I make you the CEO."

"That's what I call a vote of confidence, Mr. Tompkins."

"It's more than a vote of confidence, Mr. Carpenter. You go out there and straighten out the mess, and you'll be sitting here in two years. I guarantee it."

"Wow," he said again, letting the message sink in before saying, "I think that's an offer I can't refuse. All I have to do is convince Kimberly."

"I'm sure you can do that."

Lance stirred in his seat. "You know, there's something I should tell you before I go."

"And what's that?"

"Christine Duncan and I were classmates at Boulder High School. We went out a few times during my junior year, but it didn't work out."

The chairman threw his head back and laughed. "Did you think I didn't know that, Lance?"

"There was no reason for you to know, sir."

"I know *everything* about my senior executives, and when you told me Denver should be closed, that's when I knew you have what it takes to become the CEO of this company. Now start working on a corporation-wide transition plan that has a new executive VP in Denver by October first of next year. We'll hold off making any announcements until after the board meeting in July. With everything I see happening in global financial markets, we need to be proactive."

The next few weeks were very difficult for the Carpenters. Lance worked exclusively on developing the Diversified Global Investment Bank transition plan that downsized Denver, realigned managing director positions and regional offices, and established triggers for more draconian changes in operations and investment strategy. Though not discussed at work or at home, the assumption was that Lance would replace Christine Duncan in Denver sometime next fall, depending upon many factors, including the overall health of the financial markets and Christine's performance. Lance had agreed to structure the corporation's strategic plan and to "think" about moving to Denver, but in his mind there had still been no decision. Since the weekend he brought up closing the Denver office and then watched the Boston College quarterback throw three interceptions in the Florida State game, his stomach rumbled and demons from his past stirred his spirit whenever he thought about returning to Colorado—alone.

Kimberly started working full time as an attorney at Wiley, Young and Browne, LLP, a firm with seventy lawyers specializing in corporate finance law. Her six figure starting salary helped with their two daughters still in college. Most importantly, she filled her days with interesting work that she found challenging and intellectually satisfying. She scaled back on volunteering, but she and Lance stayed engaged with activities at both Boston University and Boston College. They attended the Eagle's final home game of the season as well as the ACC Championship game in Jacksonville and a bowl game in Orlando during the holidays. At each of the games, Kimberly sensed Lance's detachment. His mind seemed to be somewhere else, perhaps drifting to the past or shifting to the future. She only knew that since she had started back to work full time and told Lance she would not be moving to Colorado, things had been different between them.

After the first of the year, both Lance and Kimberly began adjusting to their new work routines. Lance kept an open mind on the possibility of taking over the Denver office, even if it meant a year of separation from his family; Kimberly also softened her position, knowing what an impact her adamant refusal to move had had upon their relationship.

A summer visit in Camden and a week of vacation in the Bahamas gave them much needed time together, and by August, Lance and Kimberly Carpenter were ready for the trip to Colorado for Lance's thirty year reunion—and his mission to inform Christine Duncan that her work in Denver was over.

CHAPTER SEVEN

~

At ten o'clock on Thursday morning, J. Paul Tompkins' personal Gulfstream 200 rolled down the runway for takeoff from Logan International Airport en route to the Rocky Mountain Metropolitan Airport, a major corporate reliever to Denver International Airport about halfway between Boulder and downtown Denver. On board were four people – a crew of two pilots plus Lance and Kimberly Carpenter.

The aircraft was one of three company jets owned by Diversified Global Investment Bank, and the only jet used exclusively by the chairman. He had designed the exterior paint scheme and the layout of the personal space in the cabin, including the style and color of the leather seats, the carpet on the floor—even the deep-grained, laminated wood used for interior doors, tables and wainscoting along the walls.

As soon as the aircraft began climbing to cruising altitude, Lance reached down and pulled a laptop from his briefcase, then placed it gently on the table in front of him.

Kimberly sat in the seat on the opposite side of the cabin and leaned forward to look out an oval shaped window while she held a copy of *Vogue* magazine on her lap. She had dressed for comfort knowing she faced a five-hour flight to Denver, a three-hour wait while Lance met with people in the regional office, and a short flight to Vail, the day's final destination. Even in the comfort of the JP's luxurious Gulfstream, it was going to be a long day.

Lance slipped a travel mug of coffee from a rail of cup holders attached to the side wall. He took a sip and held the mug in his left hand while he reached across the aisle and tapped Kimberly lightly on the forearm.

She sat back and turned her attention to Lance. He looked casual and comfortable with no tie and an open-collared, light blue shirt. "This is pretty neat, isn't it?"

"It's the only way to go. Sure beats dragging bags through a crowded airport ... getting half undressed going through security ... having someone next to you fall asleep and start snoring with their mouth hanging open."

"Is that what I do?"

"No, dear, but I've had that happen before."

Lance grinned and said smugly, "That doesn't happen when you're flying first class."

Kimberly looked down at the cover of her magazine. "Now don't go getting uppity with me, Lance Carpenter."

Lance gently squeezed, then released, his fingers from her forearm and felt the soft leather of his reclinable seat. Looking around the richly-appointed cabin, he responded, "I'm not getting uppity, sweetheart. I'm just thinking this is a very nice way to travel. The chairman's private jet."

"You'll get no argument from me."

"These seats recline if you want to lie back and close your eyes. It's a long flight."

"And miss all this excitement?" she said with a grin.

As they talked, one of the pilots approached from the cockpit behind them. She waited politely until they noticed her, and then she stood in the aisle facing the two passengers. "Good morning. How's the flight so far?"

"It's great," Kimberly said.

"Have you flown on this aircraft before?"

"One time for me," Lance answered. "It's the first time for Kimberly."

"Very well. I'll be in the cockpit and we'll leave the door open. If there's anything we can do for you, just let us know and we'll help as soon as we can."

The pilot wore dark blue slacks and a long-sleeved, light blue shirt with epaulets and a tie that matched the color of her slacks. Kimberly guessed she was in her late twenties and that she stood about five feet, four inches in her soft soled oxfords.

"How long have you been a pilot?" she asked, her curiosity and admiration obvious by her tone and facial expression.

"Since I was fourteen," the young pilot said. "I got my private pilot license when I turned seventeen, and then I went to Embry Riddle in Daytona and got my commercial, instrument and instructor pilot ratings. I've been flying this aircraft for ..." She stopped mid-sentence and rolled her eyes as if she were trying to remember how long. "One week!"

When Kimberly's eyes narrowed, she quickly added, "But I've got almost 500 hours in the Gulfstream 200, so you're in good hands. Between the two of us, we have more than a thousand hours flying this bird. It's a great plane and I'm sure you'll enjoy the flight. Can I get you anything before I return to the cockpit?"

"No, thank you, we're fine. We're both low maintenance travelers."

"By the way, if either of you want to sit up front in a pilot's seat, you're welcome to do that. One at a time, of course."

Immediately Kimberly said, "I'll take advantage of your offer. I've always wanted to fly."

"You never told me that," Lance added.

"You never asked."

"I'll come back to let you know when it's your turn," the pilot said with a wide smile. "We can have the women up front while the men relax in the cabin."

"If you think I can relax with two women in the cockpit, you're nuts," he said mockingly.

"Lance Carpenter, shame on you! What would your daughters say?"

"I better get back. Just let me know when you're ready to fly." The pilot flashed a thumbs-up signal to Kimberly as she returned to the cockpit.

"You'll enjoy sitting in the cockpit. They'll let you fly it, but they watch you like a hawk." Lance reflected on his one-time flying experience. Then he opened his laptop and pressed the startup button.

"You've always wanted to fly?" he asked with curiosity. "Maybe you should take some lessons. It's never too late to learn."

She nodded and smiled. "Maybe someday. But for now I'm concentrating on sharpening my legal skills." She opened her magazine and waited for her chance to fly the corporate jet.

Lance began working on his laptop and buried his thoughts in preparation for the meeting with Christine Duncan and the office staff in Denver. When he finished reviewing their fiscal operations and internal memoranda, he shut down the computer and put it back in his briefcase. Then he pulled a silver lever on the arm of his seat and lay back as the leg rests extended. Lance closed his eyes, and his mind recalled a night with the person he once knew as Christine Tanner. It had happened more than thirty years ago.

Lance drove his '73 Chevy pickup slowly over the bumpy dirt road, looking laid-back and casual in his baggy walking shorts and T-shirt.

Christine sat closely by his side, her left hand resting on his bare thigh. She felt hard muscle as she gently stroked the skin, playfully pinching his soft leg hair between her fingers as he divided his attention between driving and the hot body sitting next to him.

About a quarter of a mile from the highway, he turned into a driveway overgrown with scraggly trees and bushes. He stopped the truck and turned off the ignition and headlights. With the doors locked and windows rolled up, they were alone in the darkness. The radio played softly.

"Skooch over, Christy," he whispered even though there was no one within miles. "I'm tired of holding this damned steering wheel."

Christine pushed away and slid across the seat, her back to the passenger side door. "So what is it you want to hold?" she asked coyly.

"I think you know," he said as he rolled to her and worked an arm behind her back. With one powerful move, he pulled her against his chest and wrapped his other arm around her, too. Christine's head rested on his shoulder, and he held her tightly. "I've been wanting to do this all night."

"Do what?"

"Hold you close."

"Closely," she whispered, her lips touching his ear.

Lance pulled his head away to see her face, her impish smile barely visible in the glow of the radio dial. "What is this, you stinker, an English lesson or a night of passion on the mountain?"

"It's whatever you want it to be, Lance. What do you want?"

He didn't answer. Instead, he kissed lips that parted instantly. Her tongue flicked the tip of his, and their mouths locked together as four arms and hands began holding … and moving … and caressing. Christine pressed her breasts against his T-shirt.

When Lance felt the two mounds of flesh on his chest, he held her tighter with one arm while he kneaded the small of her back with his free hand.

Christine reached between his legs and under his shorts.

"Whoa," he said, their mouths parting for the first time in minutes. Breathing heavily, he added, "We should slow down a bit."

"Why?" She kissed him again, her fingers inching near his crotch.

Without answering, Lance moved his hand upward from the small of her back to a ticklish spot on her side.

Instinctively, she twisted away, and their chests separated long enough for Lance's left hand to cup her breast.

Christine groaned in his mouth as she rolled her breast in his grip.

Breathing heavily, they kissed and fondled each other, their clothes preventing the most intimate touch.

With their tongues still dancing in each other's mouths, Lance pulled her blouse from her skirt, and she reached for his belt buckle.

"This is moving way too fast," Lance said, sitting up and pulling away.

"Too fast? We've been dating for three months, Lance."

"I know, but we could get carried away and ..."

"And what?"

Lance looked at her while he brushed a lock of light blonde hair away from her face. "Well, we could do something we really shouldn't do."

Christine placed a hand on his cheek and rubbed it gently with her thumb. "There's nothing we really shouldn't do," she said softly. "Being with you makes my body ache. I'm about to explode inside, and I want you, Lance. I was hoping tonight would be the night." She waited for him to say something, and when he didn't, she leaned forward and pecked him lightly on the lips.

He hugged her gently as he slid his hand beneath her blouse and fumbled with the clasp of her bra.

"You don't have much experience with this, do you?" she asked softly.

"Not really," he admitted as Christine raised her arms and he awkwardly reached around her body with both hands to unhook the bra.

"It's okay. There's a first time for everything." Acting as if nothing had happened, Christine wrapped both arms around his neck and began kissing him again.

Within seconds, Lance touched her bare breast, his fingers finding the nipple firm and supple. He gently kneaded the breast and lightly circled her nipple with his fingertip.

"Oh, Lance, you have a nice touch," she whispered. "You can touch me anywhere." She slid down on the seat and spread her legs.

With his heart pounding, Lance put his hand on the inside of Christine's leg and slowly moved it higher. When his fingers felt her warm, wet panties, he placed his palm between her legs and began massaging the area.

Christine gasped and said, "Ohhh, that's good." Rhythmically, she braced against the seat and pressed against his hand. "I want you inside me, Lance," she groaned. "Please ... take me now."

Lance tensed up when he heard those words. Slowly he removed his hand from between her legs and pulled her skirt back down. "No! I can't, Christy. I'm sorry. I think we've gone way too far already."

"You can't do this to me," she screamed. "Don't do this to me!"

"I'm so sorry," he said as he straightened in the seat and reached for the key in the ignition.

"Lance, dear," Kimberly said shaking him on the shoulder. "You're sorry for what?"

Lance opened his eyes and looked around the cabin. He looked at his wife and said sheepishly, "I must've drifted off."

"You've been sleeping for almost an hour. I've been up front flying this aircraft. What a blast!"

"Was I talking in my sleep?"

"No, but you must've been dreaming or something."

"It was more like a nightmare," he said, recalling the last time he and Christine had been together. Lance glanced at his watch and turned to the window. "Looks like we're almost there. I can see mountains in the distance—and we're due to land in about thirty minutes."

"I'm ready to plant my feet on the ground. It's been a long flight, but I had a good time in the cockpit."

"Good. And apparently I got some well deserved rest."

"Yes, and that should make you fresh for your meeting this afternoon with Christine Duncan."

Lance replied with a deadpanned expression, "I can hardly wait. We've got miles to go before we sleep."

Thirty minutes later, the Gulfstream 200 touched down at Rocky Mountain Regional Airport and taxied to parking at the Denver Air Center, where two cars and personal escorts from the local office were waiting.

For Kimberly Carpenter, it would be the beginning of a Colorado adventure.

For Lance, it marked a return to a place where demons dwelled.

CHAPTER EIGHT

≈

C hristine Duncan paced back and forth in her private office waiting for Lance Carpenter to arrive. The escorts she had sent to the airport reported the plane had landed on time. Kimberly Carpenter had gone to the Flatirons Mall to kill some time; Mr. Carpenter was en route and would be in their Denver office by two o'clock.

She had awakened several times during the previous night, unable to sleep because of the impending meeting scheduled with Lance Carpenter – not only a corporate vice president, but also a bad memory from her high school days.

She gazed nervously at a grouping of small clocks on her desktop, each of them a special gift or award for outstanding performance. She bent over and pulled a hand mirror from a drawer. Staring at the reflection, she cocked her head first to the right, then the left. Christine raised her chin, and with the tip of a pinkie, she lightly dabbed her pursed lips. Then she tossed the mirror back in the drawer and slammed it shut as if she had seen a ghost.

At forty-eight, Christine Duncan still looked good, but the stress of corporate life and the scratching and clawing to get to the top had all taken a toll. Her wardrobe and accessories included the best that money could buy: tailored suits and dresses, silk scarves and a closet full of coordinated shoes and purses, many of them purchased at a thousand dollars a pop.

For the meeting today, she had chosen a solid gray suit with slacks and jacket, and a loosely-fitting, vibrant lavender blouse. From all outward appearances, she looked great.

On the inside, however, her stomach churned to the point she thought she was about to vomit. When she was informed Lance Carpenter had arrived, Christine took a deep breath and went out to meet him.

Both were smiling broadly when they met in the administrative reception area. Others stood as they watched the greetings of two high school classmates.

"Welcome back to Colorado, Lance," Christine said cheerfully, her right arm extended for a handshake.

"Hello, Christy," he said as he shook her hand, held it, and then pulled her closer for a symbolic embrace.

When they separated, she said, "It's been a long time since someone's called me Christy."

"It's been a long time since we've talked to each other," Lance said, overstating the obvious. "How long's it been? Thirty years?"

"Thirty-one," Christine countered while sweeping her arm in the direction of her office. "Shall we?"

"After you, Christy. It's your turf."

Christine rolled her shoulders back as she turned and strutted across the room with Lance following. She opened the door, invited him in, and then closed the door behind her. "Let's sit over there," she said, pointing to a small table where a colorful, animated graphic danced on a laptop screen.

"May I?" Lance asked, tugging on both lapels of his navy blazer.

"Of course. Would you like me to hang it up?"

"No, thanks." Lance slipped his arms from the blazer, folded it lengthwise, and then draped it on the back of the chair next to him.

When they had both settled into their seats, Christine said, "You look great, Lance. It really is good to see you."

Lance studied her face looking for signs of sincerity. He saw the same features that attracted him to her decades ago—a perfect complexion with rosy cheeks and seductive, pale blue eyes. "You do, too, Christine—it's probably better for me to call you Christine now—don't you think? You look good, too. That's a good color on you."

She could not stop the blush from spreading to her cheeks, but the hurt from the past controlled her emotions. She wanted to wrap both hands around his neck and strangle him, but instead she asked, "Are you going to the reunion?"

"Yes, I am. Kimberly and I are going to Vail tonight, and then we'll be driving back tomorrow. She's never been to Colorado and she wants to see the mountains up close. What about you … are you going to the reunion?"

"I signed up, but I won't be going after all." Christine looked away. "It's not public yet, but Howard and I are splitting. I'd be going alone … and besides … I don't have many pleasant memories of dear old Boulder High School. Not like some people I know."

Lance noticed her moistened eyes when she looked back. "Then I think we have something in common, Christine. Not all my memories are pleasant either, especially the last eight months. I don't think I'd be going to any reunion if it weren't for Dee Evans … and this meeting with you."

Christine seized the opportunity to go on the offensive. "You sure threw out a bombshell at the board meeting last fall," she started. "Everyone here thinks our office will be closed as some corporate cost-cutting measure. Is that what this meeting is all about?"

Lance thought a moment, then replied, "No, the office won't be closing, Christine, but I think you know it's been a tough year. Some changes need to be made."

"It's been a very tough year," she said as she pressed the arrow button on her laptop to begin her presentation. "And I'd like to show you some of the reasons why."

For the next ten minutes, Christine talked about their fiscal operations for the current year: results, trends, challenges and recommendations from her perspective. Her voice quivered from nervousness at times, and at one point in the presentation she stumbled on her own words, which contradicted the message on the screen.

Lance listened carefully without interrupting her, even when he questioned some of her conclusions. For the past eight months, ever since JP Tompkins had told him to think about taking over the Denver office, he had studied the data for all of their regional operations, and he knew where the problems were. The major problem in the Denver office was Christine Duncan—and it was Lance's job to solve it.

When she finished, Christine closed the laptop, folded her hands on the table in front of her, and breathed a sigh of relief. She waited for Lance to speak.

It was an uncomfortable silence for both of them. Lance finally spoke. "Thank you, Christine," he began formally. "I appreciate the presentation and hearing your thoughts. I know you've done everything possible to meet your annual projections."

"True," she replied softly.

"And we both know there's no way that's going to happen."

"Also true. We've already acknowledged it's been a very tough year."

Lance looked directly at Christine's empty eyes, which he thought showed a sense of hopelessness, loss, defeat. In his mind, there was no sense delaying the inevitable. "Christine, we're going to make some changes. The chairman may name a new managing director for the Denver office within the next few weeks, no later than October first."

Christine clenched her fists as they rested on the table top, and her knuckles turned white. "That's less than six weeks away," she said, her eyes filling with tears. "What are they doing with me?"

"You'll stay here through the end of the year and we'll work with you on a relocation."

"Relocation?" she asked incredulously.

"You'll have opportunities in Chicago or Boston. It depends upon who will be your replacement here. The chairman has made it clear you will have a future with DGIB."

Christine wiped away the tears with her fingers, an unsightly smear of mascara appearing under each eye. She stood up abruptly and said, "Oh, come on, Lance. I've been fired … and I'm finished! You know it and I know it. And I'm never leaving Colorado!"

"That'll be your choice, Christine, but you'll have other opportunities with the company."

"Other opportunities? It's so unfair. You have no idea what I've been through this year." Christine turned away to gather her thoughts, and when she turned back to face him, she stood with shoulders drooped, arms dangling and tears rolling down her cheeks. "You can't do this to me," she screamed. "Don't do this to me!"

"I'm sorry, Christine," Lance said calmly. "It's already done."

CHAPTER NINE

~

After the meeting with Christine Duncan, Lance asked to meet with the rest of the office staff. Twenty people crowded into a small conference room and waited patiently for the VP from Boston to arrive.

Some of the locals remembered Lance Carpenter from his glory days at Boulder High School; others had googled him after they heard about the last corporate board meeting. Even though Christine had tried to calm the storm, the rumors about closing the office ran rampant, and morale sank to an all-time low. The tension in the room was so tight, any hint of bad news could cause it to snap.

The door to the conference room was open, and Lance walked in alone. A few people stood along the walls, arms folded, some with their heads downcast. All of the chairs arranged in theatre-style rows were filled, and everyone remained seated as Lance strolled to the front of the room.

"Good afternoon, everyone," he began. "I'm certain many of you will have questions for me, and I can assure you that I will address all of them before I leave. But first, I want to stop the rumor mill, or at least slow it down." Lance smiled and looked around the room reading body language and facial expressions as he stepped closer to the people seated in the front row. Then, speaking loud enough for those in the back of the room to hear, he said with authority, "This office will not be closing. Not now ... and not in the foreseeable future."

He turned and walked slowly along the front row, waiting for his message to sink in. His eyes locked with a young man watching his every move, listening intently to every word. "There will be no additional positions eliminated, the hiring freeze will be lifted, and we see no further draconian cost-cutting measures. Everyone in this room is an important member of the team, and we've got a lot of work to do. I say 'we' because we're all in this together—everyone on the Diversified Global Investment Bank team has a lot of work to do.

"I just met with Christine Duncan and we talked about leadership changes. Her replacement, to be named by the chairman before the end of the year, will assume responsibility for this office on January fifteenth. Christine is still in charge here and will continue to serve as the managing director through the end of the year.

"As for the future, everyone at the corporate level in Boston believes the future of Diversified Global Investment Bank is bright. We've been through tough times before, and we've always managed to come through them with flying colors. And that's exactly what the chairman and the board of directors expects to happen this time. They're looking at twelve to eighteen months of belt tightening, and then, hopefully, when the recessionary pressures are relieved and the global economy takes off, we'll have more opportunities than challenges."

When Lance finished his remarks to the group, he walked back to a lectern where a glass of water had been placed for him. With his back to his audience, he drained the glass and wiped his mouth. Turning back, he laughed and said, "I've forgotten how dry it gets around here. That Colorado water sure tastes good! Now, I'd be happy to answer your questions."

Lance spread his blazer and placed both hands on his hips, waiting for the first question. When no one spoke up, he wondered whether they had bought what he said. "Here's your chance. I'll stay as long as anyone has a question, and if someone wants a few minutes to talk one-on-one, that's okay, too. When we're finished, I'm taking my wife to Vail. She's a New Englander and has never been west of the Mississippi."

Finally, a man leaning on a side wall, arms still folded, asked with a tinge of sarcasm, "If Duncan's still in charge, why isn't she in here with you?"

"To be honest, she's disappointed that she'll be leaving, and I thought it would be best for me to meet with you alone, to give you an opportunity to be heard without any fear of recrimination."

"Has she been fired?" someone else asked bluntly.

"No, the chairman has made it clear that she'll have other opportunities within the firm. They'll be talking about that over the next few weeks."

A woman in the second row raised her hand, and Lance nodded at her. "We've heard that you'll be the one to take her place. Would you care to comment?"

Lance chuckled as if he had expected to be asked that question, then he responded, "Again I'll be straight with you. Mr. Tompkins asked me what I thought about returning to Colorado. He has not yet made a final decision, and neither have I. We should all know who will be the managing director here in Denver within the next few weeks. Until then, it's probably best not to speculate."

As Lance answered each question forthrightly, the tension in the room began to ease. Some of the folks assumed they were talking with their next boss, even though he had cautioned against guessing.

When he was certain no one had any more questions or comments, Lance summed up the session. "Well, I think we've had a very frank dialogue, and I appreciate everyone's patience," he said, pausing to scan the room one final time. "In our business, there will always be challenges and there will always be change, and we will always be better off because of it. *If…*" Lance let the word hang in the air. "*If* we pool our talents and pull together as a team. I've enjoyed talking with you, and I wish each of you the very best for the coming year."

With that, he turned to walk out of the room, waving the palm of his hand in the air as he stepped toward the door.

A spontaneous applause began and continued until he was gone.

Lance Carpenter could not help but smile as he and his driver got in the car and headed back to the airport.

* * *

Christine Duncan remained behind closed doors in her office until everyone else had gone for the day. No one had attempted to see her. Even if they had wanted to, they would not have known what to say. Nor would they have liked what they saw.

She was a mess. Distraught. Angry. For all practical purposes, she had been fired. She knew it and that's what everyone was going to think. Sure, they were going to offer her other positions in the firm, but that meant moving from Denver, and she wanted no part of that. She had to talk to someone.

First she tried to call her husband to tell him what had happened. Why she called him, she could not understand. Their marriage was over anyway. She felt relieved when there was no answer and no recorded message on his phone. Then she dialed another number.

"Hello, this is Rebecca. Sorry I missed your call. Please leave a message and I'll return your call as soon as I can."

"Damn it," she said out loud, and before the recording started, she hung up. A moment later, she keyed the next number and waited.

"Hello."

"Is this Dee?"

"Yes, Christine, it's Dee."

Her emotions had reached the boiling point, and she lashed out, "You son-of-a-bitch. You and that miserable friend of yours got me fired! It's all your fault."

"Whoa, wait a minute ..."

Before Dee could say anything more, she slammed the phone down and covered both ears with her hands as if she had heard enough.

Christine crumbled into the chair behind her desk and buried her head in both arms, face down on the hard surface, and cried until there were no more tears. She closed her eyes, trying to erase all the terrible thoughts racing through her mind. She felt as if the walls were closing in around her. *What can I do? What* **should** *I do?*

There were no answers.

After a few minutes of hopelessness, Christine opened her eyes and gazed aimlessly at the precious clocks arranged on her desktop. She reached for the nearest one and read the inscription on a brass plate under the timepiece. *Outstanding Performer—2005—Thanks For Your Service.*

Slowly she stood up behind her desk, and with all the fury she could muster, cocked her arm and hurled the clock across the room. Her scream muffled the sound of glass shattering as the clock exploded against the wall.

She grabbed another clock and smashed it on top of her desk, the pieces flying in all directions.

Before she could grab the next one, the telephone rang.

"Christine, did you just call me?"

"Rebecca?"

"Yes. I saw I missed your call. Sorry, we're working on the reunion."

"I know." Her voice cracked with emotion.

"We've got a great turnout. It'll be great to see you."

"Well, that's why I'm calling, Rebecca. I'm not going to make the reunion."

"You're not? How come? I've got you and Howard sitting at the same table with me and Charles and guess who—Lance Carpenter and his wife."

Christine closed her eyes and clenched her teeth. She took a deep breath and calmly said, "You know, Rebecca, that's nice, but I never want to see that son-of-a-bitch again. And that goes for Dee Evans, too!"

"Why? What's going on?"

"Evans has made my life miserable for the past six months, and I just saw Lance Carpenter this afternoon … he fired me," she said, the tears again beginning to flow.

"Carpenter fired you?"

"My life is ruined," she sobbed. "I'm finished. All because of him. You tell him I said thanks for everything."

"Christine?" Rebecca said. "Are you okay?"

With her chest heaving uncontrollably and arms trembling, she held the receiver at arm's length and stared at it. Carefully she placed it back on the console and sat down in the chair behind her desk.

When she finally calmed her emotions, Christine Duncan reached for her purse by the pedestal of her desk. She placed it on her lap and leaned against the back of the chair.

Then she slipped her hand into the purse, wrapped her fingers around the handle of a pistol and closed her eyes.

CHAPTER TEN

≈

After a short flight to the Eagle County Regional Airport thirty-five miles west of Vail, the Gulfstream pilots helped the Carpenters load their luggage into the back of a 2008 Cadillac Escalade. Lance and Kimberly thanked them for all they had done, and soon they were headed eastbound on Interstate 70.

At Exit 176, a sign with a diagonal arrow pointed to Vail Village, and Lance angled right in the direction of a roundabout. He followed a winding road along the base of the mountain to a small, wooden welcome shack named Checkpoint Charlie, about fifty yards from the entrance to the Sitzmark Lodge. The security guard told him to pull forward and park behind another car while they registered. Overnight parking for guests was under the hotel, the entrance to the garage right around the corner.

"This is quaint," Kimberly said as she stood watching pedestrians strolling along Gore Creek Drive, a wide cobblestone street closed to vehicular traffic that weaved through the complex of businesses and shops known as Vail Village. Some couples walked arm in arm; others followed their kids dashing about in front of them.

"Let's get checked in and freshened up, and find a good restaurant with a bar. I'm famished, and I could use a drink."

"I'm for that, my dear," she said as she hooked her hand on his arm. They walked under an architectural canopy to the front door of the lodge.

Kimberly checked out the library near the front desk while Lance signed the guest register. When she returned to his side, she heard the familiar sound of his Blackberry pinging.

"You don't have to answer that," she said disdainfully. "You're on vacation now."

"It's a text message," he said as he pulled the device from his coat pocket and read the screen. "It's Dee Evans. He wants me to call him when we get to Colorado."

"Well, here we are … in Colorado."

"I'll call him when we get to Boulder tomorrow," Lance said, returning his Blackberry into a front pocket. "There's an elevator at the end of the hallway. Our room has a mountain view. That should be nice."

"We don't have much unpacking to do. We're only staying one night, and right now all I want to do is get settled. We've been on the move all day long, and I'm tired. And now *I'm* hungry, too."

After a long wait for an elevator barely large enough for two passengers and their luggage, they squeezed in and punched the button for the third floor. Kim hung her purse over one shoulder and a travel bag over the other while Lance led the way, pulling the suitcases behind him, the wheels having a mind of their own.

"Here 'tis," he said, slipping the plastic key card into a gold receptacle on the door.

When the green light on the lock illuminated, Kim opened the door, walked in and tossed her bags on the bed. "Excuse me," she said as she inched past Lance and the bags, hurried to the bathroom and closed the door.

He rolled the luggage against the wall at the foot of a king size bed. Then he opened the sliding glass door to a balcony shared with the adjoining room. Their room overlooked a spa deck on the roof of a one-story wing of the lodge. The outdoor spa featured an elevated hot tub enclosed by a slatted fence about four feet high. A collection of chaise lounges, patio chairs and tables with beige umbrellas filled the deck around a small swimming pool. Lance was leaning against the balcony railing taking in the scene when Kimberly joined him.

"This is a nice room, dear. The bathroom's spotless and they've got all the amenities."

Lance nodded to acknowledge and then he pointed to the hot tub. "Look there, Kim. We can jump in the Jacuzzi after dinner. You know, take a glass of KJ and soak our bodies in the hot, steamy cauldron. Wonder what time it closes."

"I wonder what time the restaurants close. It's almost seven o'clock. Have you decided where we're going to eat?"

Lance straightened and turned to face her. "The young gal at the front desk recommended the Left Bank restaurant. It's right downstairs and we can go like this."

"Hotel food? Why can't we find some nice, intimate place where we can have a nice conversation over couple of cocktails, a scrumptious dinner, a decadent dessert—and then we can see where that leads us."

"Are you setting a trap for me?" Lance asked. He placed his hands on her shoulders, drew her to him and kissed her softly on the lips. "From what I heard, I think the Left Bank will be perfect. It has a French and Mediterranean cuisine—and a chocolate soufflé to die for."

"Now you're talking, Lance Carpenter. Let's go."

A few minutes later, Lance and Kimberly walked through the arched doorway of an unpretentious foyer into the Left Bank's handsomely appointed bar room, where two bartenders waited to serve someone, anyone. Both wore black slacks, formal white shirt and a black bow tie; the one standing by a row of empty bar stools wore a bright crimson vest with two vertical rows of brass buttons in front. With one hand resting on the highly polished oak bar and the other on his hip, he greeted the Carpenters. "Good evening. Welcome to the Left Bank. Will you be dining with us this evening?"

"We didn't make a reservation," Lance replied, surveying the dining room and an empty bar. "But it looks like you're not too busy tonight. Can we get our drinks in the dining room?"

"Of course. The hostess will seat you, and I'll bring your drinks to your table. What would you like?"

"I'll have a Glenlivet on the rocks and the lady will have a Manhattan. And I'd like to see your wine list," Lance said as he studied a wall of built-in racks and shelves displaying bottles of vintage wine and champagne behind glass doors.

"Very well," he said graciously. "The hostess has our menu and wine list, and I will bring your cocktails to the table."

Lance and Kimberly followed a tall, string bean of a girl through a room of empty tables, all set with white linen tablecloths, fine china and silverware. Only six patrons were in the dining room – a couple seated at a table along a wall of picture windows and four others at a table in the far corner of the dining room.

"Will this be acceptable?" the hostess asked with a thick accent.

"This is lovely, thank you," Lance said, sliding an oak chair away from the table for his wife.

"Yes, this is very nice," Kim added, her tone ringing with appreciation.

"That's Gore Creek, and our regular customers love to sit by the window so they can see it. We're usually packed for dinner, but there's some big reception in town and it's been very slow this evening. Is this your first visit to the Left Bank?"

"Yes it is. We're from Boston," Lance said, looking at his wristwatch, "where it's almost ten o'clock, and we're *very* hungry."

"Boston? I've never been to Boston," the hostess said excitedly. "I'd love to see Boston someday. I've read so much about it."

Kimberly smiled at the young hostess who cradled leather bound menus and the wine list in her arms while waiting for Lance to take his seat. "I guess that makes us even, because I've never been to Colorado. By the way, you have a very interesting accent. What's your heritage?"

When Lance and Kimberly were both seated, the hostess handed each of them a menu. "I'm from Russia. I'm here on a working visa, and I love your country. I want to see as much of it as possible before I go back home. Would you like to see the wine list?" she asked, holding it at arms length for Lance, who nodded, took it and immediately began scanning the list of wines.

"I think we'll have the 2003 *Pinot Blanc,*" Lance said pointing to the selection as he spoke. "What part of Russia?"

"St. Petersburg," she answered. "Have you ever been to Russia?"

Lance shrugged and Kimberly said, "I've never ventured far away from New England."

"I am certain you will enjoy your stay in Vail. I will get your *Pinot Blanc* and give you some time to look over the menu. Everything is fantastic, and if you have any questions, just let me know." She turned away as the bartender arrived and placed their drinks on the table.

"Cheers," Lance said, holding his cocktail above the table.

"To our first night on vacation," Kimberly offered, clinking her glass against his.

"I'll drink to that." Lance tipped his glass and swallowed a full mouthful of scotch. "Whatcha going to have?"

"I don't know, but I'm thinking about trout or salmon. How 'bout you?"

"Filet. I'm sure they'll have a filet," he said, running his index finger down the list of entrees. "Yeah, here it is. Beef filet, rolled in crushed white peppercorns with a cognac sauce. That sounds really good."

"I'm going to have the fresh grilled salmon with béarnaise sauce on the side," Kim added. "And I'm going to save room for the chocolate soufflé."

"Why not. We might as well let it all hang out. After all, we're on vacation. Right?"

"Right!" Again they clinked their glasses together and beamed lovingly at each other, while a glint of moonlight reflected from the running waters of Gore Creek.

"This really is a delightful setting, Lance. They've done a wonderful job of decorating their dining room. I like the way they've coordinated the fabric in the draperies and the seat cushions with the colors in the paintings."

"You always notice those things." Lance took note of the green and white checkered curtains bundled above the window by their table and then looked around the room. "That actually looks like an art gallery," he said, pointing to an area at Kimberly's back.

Without turning her head, she asked, "Do you know what kind of parakeet that is?"

"Where?"

"The big one over my left shoulder."

Lance's eyes focused on a painting that could be seen by everyone entering the dining room. "No, but it sure is colorful."

"It's a Rosella," Kimberly said, pleased with herself that she had studied the painting as they walked to their table, and that she knew what kind of parakeet it was.

"Really?"

"To be more precise, it's a Golden Mantled Rosella, a parakeet native to Australia."

"You never cease to amaze me," he said with admiration. "And do you know what?"

"No, what?" she responded.

"I love times like this."

"Like what?"

"Like looking at a beautiful woman. Like spending a whole day with you. Like finding out you know what a Rosella is. Like knowing how much I love you."

Kimberly blushed when she heard the words. "Oh, Lance, I love you, too. I *really* do love you."

"It's been a long time since we've had a night to ourselves. With no clients, no alumni, just the two of us."

"I know. It took your thirtieth reunion and a business trip to get us out here."

"I wasn't expecting either of those to happen," Lance said resignedly. "I thought I'd *never* return to Colorado, especially for a reunion with classmates."

"You've said that before, dear, but I still don't understand why you feel that way. Most people look forward to their high school reunions."

"You know that for a fact?"

"No, but I think it's basically true. People are curious about who's coming back, who's doing what, who married whom, what happened to so-and-so. You know, your classmates will be interested in whatever happened to Lance Carpenter. Who'd he marry? What's he doing now?"

"I know at least one classmate who wants no part of Lance Carpenter."

"And that would be Christine Duncan?"

"Bingo."

Kimberly set her Manhattan glass on the table and said, "Here comes our food, and I want to savor every bite."

Lance reached for her hand and said, "Me, too. By the way, when did you learn about parakeets?"

CHAPTER ELEVEN

～

After a scrumptious dinner and a marvelous chocolate soufflé, Lance and Kimberly returned to the bar room and took a seat by a window overlooking another stretch of Gore Creek. Floodlights atop tall light poles shone on a couple sitting arm-in-arm on a wooden park bench, watching the rippling waters tumble over boulders in the creek.

When Kimberly saw a couple kissing on the park bench below, she said, "This turned out to be the perfect place. Quiet, romantic. It was an awesome dinner, and I loved the soufflé."

Lance reached for her hand and their fingers interlaced. "It's been a long day, my dear."

"A lovely day."

"Decaf?"

Kimberly nodded, and the bartender filled both of their cups.

"An interesting day, too. I got an earful about one of your old girlfriends."

"Christine? She really wasn't a girlfriend. We only went out a few times during my junior year. You know, I really didn't date that much in high school. I was more interested in sports."

"You dated during your senior year, didn't you?"

"Yeah, I dated Jessica Malone during football season and then Rebecca Carlin in the spring. Both of those were pretty rocky experiences."

"You must've been saving yourself for me."

Lance smiled for an instant, and then his features hardened. "You know I've said I wasn't looking forward to coming back to Colorado, but I've never told you why I feel so strongly about that."

Kimberly sipped her coffee and cradled the cup in the palms of her hands, and with a tilt of her head invited him to continue.

"There's something I've needed to tell you for a long time, and I've never been able to find the right time. There're some things you need to know before we start meeting people at the reunion tomorrow. Some things I wish had never happened."

Lance stared out the window at Gore Creek. Then he looked at the wall of vintage wine and champagne bottles displayed behind glass doors. Slowly, he straightened the silverware and shifted the empty bowl in the middle of the table. When his eyes finally locked with Kimberly's, he began.

"Some things happened a long time ago. Some things that burden me even today. I've tried with all my power to bury them, but no matter how hard I try, they sometimes bubble to the surface."

"You're talking in riddles, Lance. For goodness sakes, spit it out."

"Kimberly, please try to understand. What I'm telling you has haunted me for thirty years ... even longer ... my whole life, for Christ's sake."

Kimberly Carpenter had known Lance for twenty-nine years, had been married for twenty-seven of them, and she had never sensed such uncertainty before. After letting his words sink in, she finally said, "Lance, you know I love you, and I know you love me. If there's something you have to tell me, then tell me. You know I'll understand."

He hesitated and then said, "I'm not so sure."

"I promise. I'll understand." Kimberly sat back in her chair. She cradled her coffee cup in both hands and waited for her husband to share his deep, dark secrets.

He began slowly, painfully, as if every word hurt. "When I was twelve, one of the priests at school asked me to stay after class. He told me I was a good person, and that I was going to be successful in whatever I wanted to do. He said he liked me and he wanted to do everything possible to help me in school. He wanted to make me happy. Wanted to make me feel good."

"Oh, no ..." Kimberly covered her mouth with her hands and her words faded away with emotion.

"Please let me finish, Kimberly."

"I'm sorry. Go on," she said, her face reflecting the pain Lance showed while struggling to tell his story.

"It went on for two years, when I was in the seventh and eighth grade. He would ask me to stay after class at school, or sometimes we would be the last to leave the church after Bible study. He would ..." Lance stopped talking and closed his eyes, his face contorted.

Kimberly simply sat stone-faced and listened, giving Lance all the time and attention he needed.

"Eventually he moved away to another state, but the memory of what he did to me still hurts." Lance looked at Kimberly, hoping to see signs of the understanding she had promised. He saw a compassionate, caring person, the woman he had fallen in love with many years ago – the woman whose love and affection had helped bury painful memories of the past.

Lance again scanned the room. The bartender in the crimson vest was busy cleaning glasses with a towel and preparing to close for the night.

"I had no idea you were abused as a child."

"I've never told anyone. Not even my parents. I know other boys have had experiences like mine. I mean, there're all kinds of disgusting things coming out now. Many dioceses of the Catholic Church are going bankrupt because of lawsuits for sexual abuse—priests are going to prison for their actions against children. Lives have been ruined because of what lecherous old men have done to young boys during a very vulnerable time of their lives. I thought I had overcome all of that ... until my senior year at Boulder High School."

Kimberly's eyes telegraphed her curiosity, but she said, "I'm still listening."

"This one's tough, Kimberly." Lance folded his hands in front of him and continued, "We had this assistant football coach, Jack MacAdams, a former star quarterback from Denver who played at Colorado State and then got drafted by the New York Giants. He and I got into a big brouhaha during the season, and it got pretty ugly. His knee whacked my quad, which really hobbled me up a few days before the big game."

"After the last practice, I'm alone in the film room, sitting on a padded training table with an ice pack on my quad, watching a reel of our opponent's last game. MacAdams comes in, talks about the game plan, and when the film ended, he turns off the projector and flips on the light. 'You're gonna do great tomorrow, Lance,' he says. 'Let's see that leg.'"

"I take the ice pack off, and the quad is red and there's still some swelling above the knee. Coach MacAdams gives a playful punch and then sits down beside me. Wraps his arm around my shoulder. When I started to get up, he wrapped his arm tighter and said, 'You need to take your mind off the game for awhile, Lance. Seems like you're getting too uptight.' I recognized that look in his eyes. He had this glazed, expectant expression on his face as he talked—and it brought back memories of Father John."

"He began massaging my leg with both hands, his thumbs working the area above my knee. 'You've still got some puffiness, but I think you'll be okay,' he said. He kept massaging my leg above the injury, and the back of his hand brushed my shorts, and he said, 'What do we have here?'"

Lance covered his face with both palms, and then, as if he were wiping away the pain of guilt-ridden shame, he continued, "I hate myself for letting him touch me, the son-of-a-bitch. I should have stopped him, and to this day I can't explain why I didn't. I don't think I'll ever know—and I don't think I'll ever be able to forgive myself."

Kim reached for his hands and held them in hers. She squeezed gently. Then her fingers lightly stroked the back of his left hand, finally coming to rest on the gold band on his finger. "You should have told me long ago. It might have helped put it all behind you. To move on with a new life. What you've told me about your past doesn't change how I feel about you. I still love you—and tomorrow I'll love you more."

Lance turned his hands so their palms touched. "You've been the light of my life, the love of my life. We've raised a family together, and we have two wonderful children who someday will make us grandparents. But whenever I'm reminded of what happened with Coach MacAdams, I get this overwhelming feeling of guilt."

"Oh, Lance, he's the one who should feel guilty. He's the one who came on to you."

"I know, Kim, but there's more to the story. After we lost that game in state playoffs, I was crushed. It was the worst game of my life. Every time MacAdams came up to me on the sidelines, I could only think about what he did to me the night before. Then a couple of weeks later, he wanted to do it again, and this time I said no. He tried anyway. He grabbed my crotch—and I hit him with my fist. The next day he comes to school with this big black eye, and my right hand is swollen, and it didn't take long for the rumors to start flying."

"He got what he deserved, and you did the right thing. He certainly got the message, didn't he," Kim said with emphasis. "It seems to me that should have been a major turning point in your life."

"In a way, it was. I told the head coach everything that had happened with MacAdams. I never told anyone else. Nobody. Rumors ran rampant, but I never told anyone why Coach MacAdams and I had fought. They assumed it was all about football and losing the big game."

Lance paused and reached for the handle of his coffee cup. He peeked in to see if any remained, and then swallowed the last of his decaf.

Within seconds, the bartender came to the table and asked politely, "Would you like anything else from the bar?"

"No, we're finished, thank you," Kimberly said, her response intended for both the bartender and her husband. "We've enjoyed our evening here at the Left Bank, and we'll recommend it to all our friends coming this way."

The bartender acknowledged with a smile as he placed the check on the table. "I'll take that whenever you're ready, sir. There's no rush."

"Thank you," Lance said to the bartender, and when he left, he turned to Kimberly and asked, "Would you like to hear the rest of the story, my dear?"

"Of course I would."

With a strained smile Lance continued, "During the last few months of high school, the rumors ran rampant. Everyone thought MacAdams and I were at each other's throats, but the fact is, I never even talked to him. Then, during a climbing club outing in Eldorado Canyon a few weeks before graduation, he disappears and they find his body at the bottom of a rocky ravine a few days later."

"Oh, my God," Kim gasped.

"I hated him, Kim. And when I heard about his death, I felt absolutely no sense of remorse. But I've always wondered if I was in some way responsible for his death. I was the one who told the head coach what he had done. It was our fighting that got him in trouble with the administration. They called it an accident or a suicide."

"Lance, there's no way you should feel responsible for what someone else does. It sounds like he was a very sick man."

"It turns out he was a very dead man. And I know you're going to hear more about Jack MacAdams at the reunion. You'll hear about our fights, you'll hear about how I lost the state championship game, you will probably hear other things about Lance Carpenter, Boulder's fallen star."

"Oh, come on, dear. You're making way too much of this. People are going to be more interested in what's happened to everyone over the past thirty years, not what went on in high school. They'll want to know what you're doing now. What's it like to live in Boston, home of the team that won four straight from their beloved Rockies."

"You're probably right, as usual."

"I'm anxious to meet your classmates and find out what they've done with their lives. I'm sure there are going to be some real characters with some interesting tales."

"That's probably true. But why do I not want to hear them?"

"I don't know, but isn't that what reunions are for?"

"I guess so, but I gotta tell you, Kim, this one is going to open old wounds. In fact, it already has."

Kimberly smiled as she pushed her chair away from the table. "You should look at a reunion as part of a healing process. My guess is that many of your classmates would trade places with you in a heartbeat. To be in your shoes, and to have *me* in their life."

She beamed as she grabbed his hand and stood up.

"Are you ready for the Jacuzzi?"

"No, but I'm ready for bed."

"Then that makes two of us," Kimberly said as they left the Left Bank for the privacy of their room on the third floor of the Sitzmark Lodge in Vail.

Tomorrow morning they would drive back to Boulder for Lance's thirtieth high school reunion, an event he thought he would never attend. Not in his wildest dreams!

CHAPTER TWELVE

≈

For the first time in a week, Lance wore something other than business attire. He looked quite comfortable and natural in faded jeans, a bulky denim jacket and well-worn Nike cross-trainers. Just for grins, beneath his jacket he wore a white polo shirt with a logo proclaiming the Boston Red Sox the 2007 World Series Champions.

Uncharacteristically, Kimberly wore the same velour slacks and matching top she had traveled in the day before. She would change for the reception and reunion activities after they unpacked at the St. Julien Hotel in Boulder.

Instead of taking the elevator at the end of the hallway, they walked together down two flights of stairs to the main floor of the lodge, then out the west door, down a set of stone stairs leading to Willow Bridge Road, named for the bridge that crosses Gore Creek. They stopped mid-bridge and peered through the trestles at the water running below through a wooded valley of pine, cedar and cottonwood trees. An occasional gust of wind blew powdery snow from the branches, dusting the chilly morning air with a touch of early winter. A few minutes later they found the Marketplace on Meadow Drive.

The indoor marketplace was crowded with tables so small there was barely enough room for plates, coffee cups and the salt and pepper shakers. All of the tables were occupied; some people ate with their jackets on, for there was still a chill in the air inside. Others had their coats and sweaters piled on empty chairs and looked as if they intended to spend the morning reading the paper and drinking coffee from Styrofoam cups.

"I wish we had more time in Vail," Lance said, spotting a couple leaving a table in the corner. As they quickly made their way to the only empty table, he continued, "We won't even scratch the surface of what's around here."

"We'll see enough, and if we really like what we see, we can always come back another time."

"You'd come back to Colorado?"

"I'll go anywhere for a vacation, as long as it's with you."

"That's nice, Kimberly, but I think we better soak up all we can on this trip, because I don't think we'll be coming back," he said, his head nodding continuously in agreement with his own statement. "And last night I told you why."

Kimberly thought for a moment and then replied, "And I told you what happened when you were in high school shouldn't matter. You've moved on with your life—and you have a wonderful life."

"But it does matter, Kim. I'm not looking forward to reviving old memories. Or seeing Rebecca Carlin … or Jessica Malone … or who knows who else may show up at the reunion?"

"Look, Lance, you're going to see your best friend who's going to be recognized for his achievements since graduation. That alone should be reason for enjoying the reunion. Your business is over—you've fired Christine Duncan—and that wasn't your decision. It was JP's."

Kimberly stared directly into her husband's eyes as she spoke, her words right on target.

"And you, Lance Carpenter, of all people, should be proud of your accomplishments. You're in line to be the CEO of Diversified Global Investment Bank, for heaven's sake. How many of your high school classmates would love to be in your position?"

"Okay. Okay. I get the message."

While they waited for their food, Lance went to the coffee bar and fixed two cups of coffee. Kimberly pulled Lance's yearbook from her shoulder bag and began flipping through the pages. When he returned with the coffee, Kimberly said, "Maybe you can tell me about some of the people we'll meet at the reunion. I brought your *Odaroloc* to look at before the reception tonight."

"How 'bout that. You see anything interesting?"

Kimberly had a finger marking a place in the Boulder High School yearbook, and when Lance asked the question, she flipped back to a page of senior portraits. "I see a handsome young man with long, curly hair covering his ears and forehead ... and wearing a very baggy, plaid shirt."

"Who's that?" Lance asked, carefully placing the hot coffee in front of her.

Smiling, Kimberly read the name and words printed under the photo. "Rhett Craddock. Most Likely to Succeed."

Lance sat down and tilted back, giving her a look of disbelief. "Rhett Craddock? I thought you were talking about me!"

"It's not always about you, my dear," she said. "Oh, here you are on the same page. Ummm ... you look handsome, too. Very hot. But you look awful serious, like you mean business or something."

"As I recall, the class photos were taken in the spring, and that was not a very pleasant time for me. After we lost in the state playoffs, things were never quite the same. I wanted to get as far away from Boulder as possible. That's one of the reasons I went to BC."

"Where you met me!"

"Yes, and thank goodness I did."

Kimberly touched the page and circled his picture with her index finger. "I remember this face, your long hair, you were really something—the Colorado cowboy. The man I fell in love with."

Lance smiled at the pleasant memory of their meeting and courtship, and then he returned to the present moment. "Rhett Craddock was my wide receiver. He was only about five-eight at best, but he was lightning fast and no one could cover him. He caught thirty or forty passes, scored umpteen touchdowns. But he never played in college. Too small, they said, but I don't think he ever wanted to go to college. I think he stayed in Boulder, but I'm not sure."

"Rebecca Carlin. Her picture is right next to yours. Isn't she the one who organized all the reunion events?"

"That's the one. She was also one of the gals I dated during my senior year."

"You mean your last love before me?"

"We only dated, Kim, and there were a few others."

"Other whats?"

"Other girls I dated … before you."

"How many?"

"Does it matter?"

"Just curious."

Lance chuckled under his breath. "Well, if you really want to know, I had three girlfriends in high school. Christine was the first and Rebecca was the last. None of the relationships worked out very well."

"I can't imagine that. Who was the third? Jessica?"

Lance nodded and sipped his coffee.

"Why didn't that one work out?"

"Oh, I don't know," Lance said, staring straight ahead. "You might see all of them tonight. Maybe you should just *ask them*."

"Sure. Why not? We may see them tonight, and then again we may not."

"We'll see Rebecca if she's the one who organized the reunion."

"Right."

"So tell me about her."

"There's nothing to tell."

"Nothing to tell?" Kimberly knew better, her female instincts reading his reluctance to talk about high school girlfriends. "You dated your senior year and you don't have anything to say about her?"

"Nope."

"Then I guess we should eat our breakfast, because our food's ready." Kimberly closed the yearbook and put it back in her bag.

"I'll get our plates," Lance said.

Talk about Lance's high school friends would have to wait.

CHAPTER THIRTEEN

B y the time the Escalade turned eastbound on Interstate 70, the sky had become overcast with dark gray clouds that stirred continuously with the brisk mountain breezes. The weather forecast called for a slight chance of snow in the afternoon, but when a few flakes began falling before noon, it looked as if the weatherman had missed again.

"My goodness, it's snowing in August," Kimberly said, looking up from the yearbook opened on her lap.

"Most of that's coming from the wind on the slopes, but it looks like we could get some more snow. Early snows are good and they really need all they can get, not only for the ski season, but also to help the drought. They had to ration water in Colorado last summer because it was so dry."

"You're sounding like a native, dear. *We* this and *we* that."

"It's true, Kim, they need snowpack in the mountains to replenish ground water supplies. Everyone in this part of the country knows that. Especially the folks in Arizona, Nevada and California," he said, shifting his perspective from we to they.

Lance began slowing down and flipped up his turn signal. "This is Idaho Springs. We could go all the way to Denver on the interstate, but I think you'll like Boulder Canyon Drive, a road I've driven a hundred times. I always enjoy it."

"Whatever you say, dear. You're the tour guide—and I'm enjoying the ride." Kimberly leaned forward and reached into her bag on the floor. She found a tube of Curel, squeezed a dab into her palm and began rubbing the lotion into her hands. "Now what about Rebecca Carlin … and what did you see in her … and why do you clam up every time you hear her name?"

"What is this … twenty questions? I told you, Kim, there's nothing much to tell. We dated. I went to Boston College. She went to Colorado State. End of story."

"I know you, Lance Carpenter. I have a feeling this is just the beginning of the story. I can't wait to meet her."

"She's worked hard pulling together all the loose ends for the reunion. Dee told me Rebecca has reached out to everyone she could find and encouraged them to come back for this weekend."

"She didn't reach out to you, did she?"

"Matter of fact, she did. But when I got the letter, I tore it up. I wasn't the least bit interested in coming back to Boulder. Not until Dee's call."

"She was attractive in high school. I wonder what she looks like now."

"Oh, yeah, she was attractive all right. I never dated anyone that wasn't a good looker."

"Thank you. I'll take that as a compliment."

"You're welcome, my love. That's what I intended it to be."

For the next hour, Lance and Kimberly talked about Lance's high school days and enjoyed driving the scenic route along Boulder Canyon from Nederland to Boulder. All traces of the snow that had fallen in the vicinity of Vail had vanished, and the gauge in the Escalade showed an outside air temperature of sixty-eight degrees. The last few miles of the highway cut through mountain passes of the Front Range, leaving steep walls of rock and craggy granite towering high above the road. Rock slides were evident at some spots, with boulders the size of beach balls resting inches from the pavement.

As they entered the Boulder city limits, Lance's Blackberry chimed. He pulled it from a jacket pocket and read the text message.

"It's Dee. He wants me to call him."

Kimberly nodded and turned her attention for her first look at Boulder, an impression that reminded her of driving through many of the charming little towns in southwestern Maine.

With a few clicks of his thumb, Lance scrolled to Dee's cell number and pressed the trackball to place the call. After several rings, he heard Dee's familiar voice answer his call.

"Good afternoon, Lance Carpenter here. How you doing?"

"Doing well, thank you. Where are you?"

"Kim and I just drove into Boulder. We flew in yesterday. I had a meeting in Dénver in the afternoon, and then we had the company jet drop us off in Vail."

"Eagle County?"

"Yeah. We picked up a car and drove to Vail. Spent the night at an Alpine lodge in Vail Village."

"The Sitzmark?"

"How'd you know?"

"That's where I always stay when I'm in Vail. Did you try the Left Bank?"

"Oh my gosh, you're right again. We had a wonderful dinner last night. Capped off by …"

"Their chocolate soufflé," he interrupted mid-sentence.

"Dee Evans, you never cease to amaze me. What are you, psychic or something?"

As they drove east on Canyon Boulevard, Lance continued talking on his Blackberry, looking for Ninth Street, where he turned north to the St. Julien Hotel.

"We're at the hotel now. It looks like a nice place. We've got two bellmen in white shirts and bow ties headed our way."

"It's a quality property. Just opened a couple of years ago. They thought about having the reunion dinner there, but it was way too expensive for our event."

When one of the bellman opened her door, Kimberly, who had been sitting quietly listening to Lance's half of the conversation, touched his arm to get his attention. "*I have to pee!*" she mouthed as she hurried through front doors. The concierge anticipated her question and gave directions to the nearest restroom.

"Hang on, Dee," Lance said, stepping out of the car. He handed the bellman the keys and pointed out the luggage that would be going to their room, then placed his cell to his ear.

"Okay, I'm back with ya."

"Very good," Dee said. "I was wondering if we could get together this afternoon. I've decided *not* to attend the welcome reception tonight, and there're some things we need to talk about before the class dinner tomorrow night. You remember where I live, don't you?"

"Do you still have the house on Knollwood?" Lance entered the lobby of the St. Julien Hotel and approached the concierge desk on his right.

"That's the one. I bought it from my parents, and I've got some university students taking care of the place when I'm in California."

"You've got to be kidding me. CU students in that house? I'll bet the neighbors love that."

"They are very carefully selected and they take good care of it, so it works well for me," Dee countered. "So can you come over this afternoon?"

"Well, Kim and I are going to browse around Pearl Street for awhile. We could stop by a little later this afternoon."

"I'd like you to come over right away," Dee quickly responded, a sense of urgency resonating in his voice.

"Why? What's up?"

After a noticeable pause, Dee said, "It's about Christine Duncan."

Lance stood near the registration counter, waiting for another guest to complete the registration process. "I saw her yesterday afternoon," he said quietly.

"I know. That's why we need to talk … and it can't wait."

Lance understood the urgency in Dee's voice, but reluctantly he said, "Okay, Dee. We'll check in, unpack our bags, and we'll be at your place in about thirty minutes."

"Good. I'll be waiting. And Lance, I'm really looking forward to seeing you."

"Me, too." Lance punched the red key and slipped his Blackberry back into a jacket pocket.

"We'll be where?" Kimberly asked as she joined him at the registration counter, a sense of relief evident on her face.

"To Dee's. He insists that we come over right away. He wants to talk about my meeting with Christine Duncan."

"And that's more important than you and me seeing Pearl Street?"

"He said it can't wait, Kim, and besides, I think you'll like seeing Dee's home. By now it's probably worth a million or more. We can check out Pearl Street tomorrow."

"Whatever. This is *your* reunion."

CHAPTER FOURTEEN

~

O n the western edge of the city, nestled high in the hills of a
greenbelt preserve owned by the county, the Evans home had a
striking view of Boulder and the plains that extend all the way
to Denver. It was an impressive residence when built in 1972, and Dee's
decision to buy the home from his parents turned out to be a good one. Not
only did it increase in value to nearly two million dollars, but it remained
his primary residence while he built his fortune in Silicon Valley.

The Evans family of three had relocated to Boulder in the mid-
sixties. The only son of two university professors, Dexter Eugene Evans
was six years old when his father joined the faculty at the University of
Colorado as a Professor of History in the College of Arts and Sciences.
They bought their first home in a modest north Boulder neighborhood,
three doors down from the Carpenters, another family of three that had
relocated from Kansas a year earlier.

Lance and Dee had become inseparable best friends during their
early childhood years. They played in the street together; they walked to
school with their lunch boxes dangling from their sides; they sometimes
argued over nothing and ended up wrestling on the ground—with
Lance always winding up on top.

The friendship developed during their childhood years, and even
when their intellectual interests and physical characteristics became
more differentiated, Lance and Dee's friendship endured.

By the time they entered Boulder High School as sophomores, it was clear that Lance Carpenter was going to be the class jock and Dexter Evans would be the class nerd, ten years before the word became immortalized by the film *Revenge of the Nerds*.

Everyone expected Lance to be the star athlete. No one noticed Dee, except when he and Lance hooked up in the courtyard or the cafeteria or showed up at a house party on Saturday night. Even then, Lance was the dominant personality, the one who attracted the attention of the ladies. Dee tried to fit in, but he was never very comfortable when the conversation focused on sports, hot chicks or hot cars, and he was accepted at school mainly because he was Lance Carpenter's best friend.

Dee's family moved into the three-story Knollwood home during the summer between Dee's sophomore and junior year at Boulder High School. From that time on, Lance and Dee became immersed in their own interests: Lance's—athletic, and Dee's—academic. Yet they remained very close friends, with Lance always standing up for Dee whenever anyone spoke unkindly of him, or made him the butt of a practical joke.

Dee's move to Knollwood also put him in a different socio-economic stratum. He was branded as an elitist, one of the rich kids from Mapleton Hill, someone born with a silver spoon in his mouth – someone who would never have to worry about being accepted, or successful, because he would have family wealth to take care of him for the rest of his life. Nothing could be further from the truth.

Yes, Dee's parents both had a decent salary as university professors. They had lived frugal lives and made a few good investments, their portfolio supplemented by a modest inheritance from Dee's last living grandparent. But they had to stretch to buy the Knollwood home, and they were intent to pay off the mortgage in fifteen years, which they did. Their only other financial goal was to ensure Dee could go to any university in the country without having to work, and with their simplistic lifestyle, they had saved enough for Dee to attend Stanford University, the school of his choice, for at least a couple of years.

"That's Dee's house on the right," Lance said turning south at the corner of Greenrock and Knollwood Drive.

"Very nice."

"I don't think he'll mind if I park in the driveway. Can you imagine getting in and out of here when it snows?"

"It's probably no worse than our place."

Lance grinned as he drove up the steep embankment and stopped in front of the wood-paneled garage door. "Oh yes, it is. I've seen cars slide right off the driveway into the street. Of course, alcohol was a factor, but in this neighborhood, it's always an adventure when it snows."

Lance flipped off the ignition and said, "Okay, dear, let's go meet Dee Evans and find out what can't wait 'till tomorrow."

Kimberly surveyed the front of Dee's home. She saw two entrances, one at ground level and the other accessible by a redwood staircase leading to an elevated deck that also served as a cover for the lower entrance. "Where do we go?" she asked, waiting for Lance to lead the way.

"Let's go up. That door goes to the downstairs recreation room. At least that's what it was thirty years ago. It was a great place for parties. Pool room, television, big built-in bar. But no one ever wanted to come to Dee's house. It was too nice ... and Dee wasn't exactly the partying kind of guy."

Lance and Kimberly climbed the stairs and rang the doorbell. Shortly, a young man opened the door and greeted them with a warm smile.

"You must be the Carpenters." He stood tall, his head tilted slightly to the side, and with an exaggerated, sweeping gesture, he said, "Please come in. Dexter will be with you in a few minutes. He's upstairs on the telephone."

Dexter? Kimberly mouthed to Lance with a curious expression on her face. She stepped inside and waited while the young man closed the door behind them.

"Oh, my! A Boston Red Sox shirt? You sure know how to rub it in.

We were so devastated when our Rockies lost," he said with a painful scowl for additional emphasis.

The young man led them to the living room with a U-shaped arrangement of a sofa flanked by love seat on each side, all with a spectacular view from picture windows overlooking the city.

"Would you like something to drink?" he asked. "We have water, soft drinks, or I can brew some tea or coffee if you'd like."

"Water would be great," Kimberly replied.

"Same for me."

"That's easy enough. And it's *soooo* good for you." With coats still tucked under his arms, the young man swirled away.

"Are you thinking what I'm thinking?" Kimberly's eyes flicked to the ceiling and then locked with Lance's as if she expected an immediate response. She glanced at the door where the young man had disappeared like a light breeze through the ribbony leaves of a weeping willow.

Before he could answer, he heard Dee's voice coming from somewhere above them.

"I'll be with you in a minute."

Lance and Kimberly turned their heads and saw Dee Evans looking down at them from a small loft that overlooked the living room. He held a cell phone to his ear and one hand rested on top of an oak railing. A skylight in the canted ceiling provided natural lighting not only for the loft, but for the living room as well.

"Is Jeffrey getting you something to drink?"

Lance nodded, "Yes, he is."

Dee acknowledged with a wave of his free hand and then began speaking into his cell phone as he turned his back to them and left the loft. A few minutes later he came down the stairs to meet Lance and Kimberly.

He was taller than Lance remembered, still gangly but significantly more muscular in the arms and shoulders. Lance stood as Dee rounded the end of the richly embroidered sofa. Graciously he extended his right arm for a handshake and embraced Lance in a half-hug with the other arm.

"It's been a long time, my friend," Dee said still gripping Lance's hand.

"We're talking thirty-plus years."

"That's a long time by any standard."

"You look great, Dee. Looks like you've taken to exercise and good nutrition."

"If you call walking to work exercise, I guess you're right," Dee said chuckling, his attention turning to the lady still seated on the sofa. "You're even prettier than I imagined, Kimberly," he said reaching for her hand. "It's good to meet you in person. Welcome to Colorado."

"Nice to meet you, too."

"I always knew Lance Carpenter would marry the right woman."

Kimberly flushed. She was about to speak, but Dee continued, "That guy was the number one prize in our class. He needed me to keep all the girls away from him."

"Oh, come on, Dee Evans, that's a bunch of BS and you know it," Lance interjected. "And Kim knows it, too."

"He was pretty hot when I met him," she said turning her head to Lance, taking exception to his self-deprecation. "I was certain there were dozens of Boston babes hoping he'd call and ask them out. That's why, when he showed some interest in me, I decided to play for keeps."

"You did? You never told me that."

"I didn't want you to know."

"Why not? I thought we agreed to share our deepest thoughts."

Kimberly flashed a coquettish grin and said, "We did, and we do, but as you well know, some things are better saved for the right moment."

Dee had taken a seat in one of the matching love seats while the Carpenters bantered back and forth. He leaned back with his legs crossed, the top one bent at the knee and moving constantly while he listened, as if he were anxious to rejoin the conversation. "Then this must be the right moment," he said. "Nothing like sharing deep, dark secrets with a complete stranger to spark the flames."

"You're not a complete stranger, Dee. I feel like I've known you for years. Lance has told me all about you."

"He has?"

"Yes, he has. He said you were the smartest guy in the class and the one most likely to be successful in business. Said you were the one in his group of friends who kept him out of trouble."

"He did?"

"There she goes again, letting the cat out of the bag," Lance said, beaming a broad smile.

"It must be the right moment ..." Dee paused when he saw the young man enter the room carrying a tray of glasses and a bowl of mixed nuts and a platter of cheese and crackers. "Because here's our refreshments."

Holding the tray above his shoulder with the palm of his hand, the young man willowed his way to the coffee table, bent down and arranged coasters in front of the threesome. Then he placed the glasses filled with ice and water, first in front of Kimberly, then Lance. On Dee's coaster he set a can of Coke, pop top already open. His final task was to make room on the coffee table for the bowl and platter, but when he removed the plate of cheese and Wheat Thins, the tray tipped and the bowl shattered on the hardwood floor, with glass, nuts and raisins scattering everywhere.

He sucked in a deep breath and said, "Oh my goodness! I am *soooo* sorry." He quickly knelt on the floor and began to sweep the mess into little piles with his hands, attempting to hide his embarrassment with well-intentioned industry.

"It's okay, Jeffery," Dee said uncrossing his legs and shifting in his seat. "Accidents happen, and it's not the end of the world."

"I'm so sorry, Dexter. Your friends must think I'm a real klutz."

"Not to worry. You can leave it for now. After all, Mr. Carpenter and I haven't seen each other for thirty years, and we've got some catching up to do before the reunion tomorrow."

"I can have it all cleaned up in no time," he insisted.

"Jeffery," Dee spoke firmly. "I said it's okay. We'll take care of it later."

With that, his shoulders drooped and his head lowered. The young man, feeling both embarrassed and scolded, turned and sulked out of the room.

"He'll be okay," Dee said. "He's a great young man that I've taken under my wing. Mentored him, encouraged him. He's like a son to me, a good kid with a very thin skin."

"Like someone I used to know?"

Dee smiled and sat back in the loveseat. He folded his hands in his lap and gently rubbed the palms together as if massaging, drying, or cleansing them. Or signaling his intention to avoid an answer and move the conversation to the primary purpose of their meeting.

"You know, Lance, I've wanted to see you ever since I found out you worked for JP Tompkins. I had hoped we could spend a lot of time catching up, but after what happened yesterday, everything has changed."

"Christine Duncan?"

"Yes, Christine Duncan. She was the person handling my IPO."

Lance puzzled. "Really? I thought you'd be working with the San Francisco office."

"It's a long story."

"Well, we've got time. After all, Dee, you're the reason we're in Colorado."

"You don't mind if we talk a little business, do you?" Dee directed his question at Kimberly, who had been listening as she scanned the furnishings and noted the décor of Dee's home.

"Not at all. I'm used to that by now," she said. "I can help clean up this mess on your hardwood floor."

"Nonsense. We'll do that later," Dee said. "I know you're both anxious to get back to the hotel, so I'll lay it out for you as quickly and clearly as I can. You see, when I decided to take my company public, I chose the Diversified Global Investment Bank because it had a great track record in IPOs. But after months of frustration and dealing with problem after problem in the San Francisco office, I got fed up and called JP Tompkins himself. He said he'd have one of his top executives contact me, and within ten minutes, I got a call from Christine Duncan. Now how ironic was that? Christine Duncan, the vivacious, curvaceous chick from Boulder High School designated to handle the initial public offering of one of her classmates, Dexter Eugene Evans, to whom she would never even give the time of day."

A hint of bitterness leaked into his words as he continued, "Here I am going public with a quarter of a billion dollar initial public offering, and she's all warm and phony—and her incompetence makes the guy in Frisco seem like a financial genius. There's another disaster in the making, so I call JP again, and he tells me he's making a change in the Denver office. He assures me he's got another top executive that he personally guarantees. The person he's chosen to replace him as CEO."

Lance sat quietly and listened, shifting slightly in his seat.

Dee reached for his can of Coke and swallowed a couple of mouthfuls of the beverage. Now smiling, and any sign of resentment gone, he continued, "So I ask JP, 'Who is your superstar?' And without hesitation he says, 'Lance Carpenter.' And I'm speechless. Absolutely dumbstruck. First Christine Duncan and now Lance Carpenter, my very best friend from Boulder High School? You talk about a Colorado irony."

"You think *you* were dumbstruck? I had no idea what your company is worth, and I didn't know you were working with DGIB."

"No reason you should have known either. I'm one of the many West Coast technology ventures that starts up, makes a little money, and then gets gobbled up by a larger firm—and smiles all the way to the bank. Your investment bank has billions in assets and hundreds of clients. No reason you should have known I was one of them."

"JP could have told me."

"JP has too many things on his mind these days."

Dee took another sip of Coke and set the can back down on the table in front of him. "Precisely. Like who's going to straighten out his Denver office, and when he's going to retire, and who will replace him as the CEO. I thought you might figure in all three of those things. Until yesterday. Now it's all up in the air, and so is my IPO. What in the world did you say to Christine Duncan?"

"Nothing she wasn't expecting. She didn't handle it very well."

Dee leaned forward, his head nodding in slow motion. "That's an understatement, Lance. "She's dead!"

Kimberly gasped; Lance sat back as if the shock had blown him away. "She's what?"

"They found her in her office this morning, and you were the last person to see her alive. She called me after you left and blamed you for all of her problems. Then she called Rebecca and told her she wouldn't be at the reunion after all. She said you and I would know why."

"Oh, my God." Lance shook his head as if to erase the negative memories of Christine Duncan. He had crushed her heart in high school and when he delivered the message that would ruin her professional life, she had screamed at him, *You can't do this to me!*

"It's going to put a huge damper on the reunion this weekend. The word is certain to leak out, and you and I are right in the middle of it. People will eventually find out that I couldn't work with her. They'll wonder if you got her fired so you could take her place in Denver."

"That's crazy, Dee. I've *never* wanted to come back to Colorado!"

"Doesn't matter. Rebecca called me right after the call from Christine, and if she tells others half of what Christine apparently told her, the rumors will begin to fly. We'll be portrayed as the villains, the ones who pushed Christine Duncan over the edge. That's why I'm not going to the reception tonight. I'll be at the Stadium Club for the dinner tomorrow night, but I won't be hanging around afterward."

"You're the guest of honor, Dee. Remember? Boulder High School's distinguished citizen of the year? We're here to share in your recognition. And from what I've learned, you've earned it."

"By the end of the evening tomorrow night, you'll probably regret coming back to Boulder."

"I think you're wrong on that one, Dee. I already do." Lance chuckled sarcastically, then continued, "But it really is good to see you, and it's great to know how successful you've been with your company—and that you'll still be working with us."

"I'm not going to be working with the Diversified Global Investment Bank. I'm going to be working with Lance Carpenter, my high school idol, the one person in the world I know I can always count on to do the right thing."

"You're very kind, Dee, but ..."

"But nothing," he interrupted. "It's true. I've always had you right up there on a pedestal, and now I want you to get the credit for taking my company public and for ensuring the success of your investment bank as a major player in the world's financial industry."

"Dee, you don't ..."

"I'm hoping you'll take the Denver office, and that ultimately you'll take JP's place at the top. We just have to make it through tomorrow night."

CHAPTER FIFTEEN

～

When Lance and Kimberly returned to the St. Julien, Lance draped his jacket over the back of a wicker chair in the TV room of their corner suite on the fourth floor. He slipped his Blackberry from a leather case and said to Kimberly, "I have to call JP. He'll want to know about Christine."

"Go ahead. I'm going to lie down for awhile."

"Good idea. I may join you in a few minutes." Lance stepped outside on the patio overlooking the Merrill Lynch building and the Boulder Chop House and Tavern.

Kimberly lay down on the right side of a four-poster king size bed. She felt as if she had been on an emotional roller coaster since they left Boston on JP Tomkins' personal airplane yesterday morning. Staring at the ceiling, she replayed the last twenty-four hours—the long flight to Denver; Lance's meeting with Christine Duncan; their dinner at the Left Bank and Lance's revelation of abuse by Father John and the incident with Coach MacAdams; making love in the darkness and quiet of their room in Vail; meeting Dee Evans and learning of Christine's death.

Kimberly sat up and gently massaged her temples. Then she stood, shuffled to the bathroom and looked at her reflection in the mirror. She did not like what she saw.

Her eyes were swollen. Her hair was matted and needed a shampoo.

Not only did she look tired, she was drained from a twenty-six-hour yesterday, and she had awakened long before sunrise in Vail, her physical clock still on Boston time.

For reasons she could not fully understand, tears were rolling down her cheeks. She finished wiping them away just as Lance appeared in the doorway. He had been sitting on the patio, mulling over his conversation with JP while Kimberly slept.

"Are you okay, dear?" he asked softly.

"I've been better."

He came to her side and slipped his arm around her waist. "I'm sorry to put you through all this, Kim. I knew it was going to be difficult at times, but Christine Duncan killing herself is a real bombshell."

"To say the least."

"Dee and I may get some of the blame, but the reality is, that woman was screwed up big time."

Kimberly eased away and reached for another tissue from a ceramic box on the counter. She blew her nose and dropped the tissue in the toilet. Without responding, she brushed past her husband as she left the bathroom.

Lance followed a few steps behind, and when she sat down on the edge of the bed, he asked again, "Are you sure you're okay?"

She looked up and said "I'm here for *your* reunion—and to support my husband while he does what he has to do for the good of the corporation. I can handle seeing all your old girlfriends, and I don't give a damn what happened thirty years ago between you and Christine, and Rebecca Carlin … or any other woman that comes up and says, 'Oh, Lance, it's so good to see you again after all these years.'"

He started to speak but was interrupted.

"What bothers me most is what you told me in Vail, and why you held it inside for all these years. Why didn't you share that with me before? What else am I going to find out about Lance Carpenter?"

"I don't know, Kim," he said throwing his arms in the air. "Nothing. That's all there is, I suppose."

"You suppose? But you're not sure."

"How do I know what's going to come up? What people are going to say? Why do you think I never wanted to come back in the first place?"

"I don't know. You never even bothered to tell me until yesterday."

He looked at her as if she had thrown a dart to the heart. "Great," he said turning away. "Now I've got something else to deal with."

Kimberly leaped up from the bed and shouted, "Deal with? You have to *deal with* me?"

"I'm sorry, Kim. I didn't mean it to sound that way."

"Well it did."

Lance came to her and gently touched her shoulders. "It's just that I know you're upset, and whenever that happens, it bothers me, too. Especially if it's something I did to upset you."

He sat down at the foot of the bed and patted a place beside him. When she sat down, he continued deliberately, "I'm *dealing with* a classmate who wants me to handle his initial public offering, a woman I dated in high school who kills herself the day I fire her, and a pissed off boss who wants me to take her place in the Denver office. That's what I'm *dealing with*."

"JP?"

"Yeah, I talked with him while you were resting."

"And?"

"He said he heard about Christine's death from someone in her office and he's pissed off that he didn't hear it from me."

"You just found out an hour ago."

"I know. But JP also said she left a note saying that after her meeting with Lance Carpenter, she could not go on living. She blasted me, Dee and the entire corporate culture of the Diversified Global Investment Bank. Then she put a bullet through her head."

"I'm sorry, Lance. I know this is difficult for you, too," Kimberly said, standing beside him with her hand resting gently on his shoulder.

Lance looked up at her. "Would you like to hear what else JP had to say?"

"Of course. I want to know everything."

"He said the people in the Denver office want me to take over, and he wants me in place by the first of October."

Ironically, as Lance relayed JP's message, the sun slipped behind a darkening cloud and the brightness in the room disappeared.

Kimberly dropped both arms to her side, and with a quiver in her lower lip, she said softly, "And if you take the Denver office, you go alone."

"I know. You've made that perfectly clear."

Kimberly managed a smile. She stood and looked down at the clothes she had been wearing for the past two days. "I better get in the shower and change into something more appropriate for the reception. It's casual, isn't it?"

"Very casual." Lance pointed to his well-worn jeans and Boston Red Sox polo shirt that he had been wearing since they left the lodge in Vail. "I may even go like this. I don't feel like hanging around the reception for hours anyway."

"Whatever you want, my dear. Remember this is *your* reunion."

CHAPTER SIXTEEN

～

For many decades the Millennium Harvest House in Boulder had been a gathering place for people attending rush week activities, parents weekends and major events at the university. However, the Harvest House was best known for its FAC, an acronym used as both a noun and a verb and that stood for Friday Afternoon Club. The FAC had become a traditional location for groups of all kinds to gather on the night before Colorado Buffalo home football games. It was also popular for university and high school class reunions.

Rebecca Carlin had polled their classmates for preferences on reunion activities. They had settled on a reception Friday night, a reminiscent tour of the high school on Saturday morning, the dinner dance would be held in the Stadium Club at Folsom Stadium, and for hardy souls wanting more time with classmates and their families, they could go to the picnic on Sunday at Central Park.

Rebecca and Suzanne Johnson, the class treasurer, had worked together on every detail of the reunion, from rates for lodging, food and beverages to the set up for check in and registration at the dinner dance on Saturday night.

The corner of the lobby inside the front entrance doors had been converted into a welcome center. A purple and gold banner on the north wall greeted the graduates and guests: Welcome Back … Class of 1978 … Boulder High School.

Pre-printed nametags, with the women's maiden names in parentheses, were neatly arranged on two 4' by 8' tables, one table for last names beginning with the letters A-J, and the other for letters K-Z. On the floor behind the tables were three boxes packed with welcome packets for each of the attendees.

Rebecca stood beside the A-J table where she could see everyone before they came through the glass doors at the entrance to the hotel. When she recognized Lance, she stopped dialing a number on her cell phone and waited for the Carpenters to enter the lobby.

"Rebecca?" Lance said when he saw her standing by the tables. She was a tall woman, about five nine in flats and pushing six feet in heels, which meant she could almost look at Lance eye to eye. Her hair was a natural dark brown, almost black, with a few strands of silver beginning to show. At first glance, Lance thought she looked more slender than the last time he saw her. But that was a memory he had tried to erase.

"That would be me, Lance Carpenter. Welcome back to Boulder."

Lance extended both arms and wrapped them around her in a momentary, symbolic embrace. "Good to see you, Rebecca. It looks like the years have been very good to you. This is my wife, Kimberly."

"It's nice to meet you, Kimberly. Welcome to Boulder."

"Thank you. It's good to be here. My first time in Colorado."

"You picked a good time to be here. We've got a great turnout for the reunion, and I'm sure you'll enjoy meeting some of your husband's classmates."

"Matter of fact, we saw Dee Evans at his home earlier today, so the reminiscing has already begun."

Rebecca straightened and said, "Really? I was about to call him when you came in. He called a few minutes ago, and I missed the call. We've been scrambling to get things ready for registration and the reception tonight." Turning to Lance, she continued, "By the way, do you remember Suzanne Johnson?"

Lance looked at the woman standing behind the K-Z table, and after a moment's pause, he nodded his head in her direction and said,

"Of course I do. How could I forget the gal who sat beside me in Mr. Cooper's math class?"

"She's the catering manager here at the hotel, and she's helped grease the skids for a great reunion."

"Hey, Suzanne, good to see you."

"Back at ya, Lance. We're glad you're here. We've got a hundred people signed up for the Friday night reception and another hundred for the dinner tomorrow night."

"It should be interesting," Lance said unconvincingly. "I'm here for Dee Evans. He convinced me I should come."

Rebecca immediately responded, "You mean you didn't come back to see *us*?" She held both arms outward with the palms of her hands facing the heavens. "That hurts our feelings, but as I remember, you've done that before." Rebecca put on a fake frown and pretended to pout.

Lance grabbed Kimberly's arm, turned to the door and took a couple of quick steps, pretending to be offended. "Okay, that does it. We're outa here!" Then he stopped abruptly, and with a warm, personable grin, returned to the registration table. "You've done a great job with the planning, Rebecca. Great Panther banner."

"There's a list of attendees and a schedule of events in the welcome packet. There are also six pages of recent photos that people sent in, but we didn't get one from you."

"You know, I didn't think we'd make it, but Dee called and twisted my arm. Thank goodness you've got nametags for everyone."

"*You* won't need a nametag, Lance. Everyone will remember you. My goodness, you haven't changed at all." Rebecca's smile had hardened, her words tainted with sarcasm.

"I'm not so sure."

"Not so sure about what? Everyone will remember you or you haven't changed at all?"

Lance recalled Dee's warning: *If she tells others half of what Christine apparently told her, the rumors will begin to fly.* "Both," he said as he scanned the array of nametags, looking for his and Kimberly's.

Rebecca walked behind the table. She reached for the two Carpenters and picked them up, one in each hand. "Here's yours, Kimberly," she said with a pleasant smile. Then, still managing to smile, she held Lance's nametag in front of him and said, "I talked to Christine Duncan yesterday."

"So did I."

"I know."

Lance peeked at his nametag and slipped the plastic holder into his jacket pocket. "It was a business meeting."

"That's what she told me. She said you fired her."

Suzanne Johnson was not part of the dialogue, but she inched over, cocked an ear and listened intently to every word.

Kimberly tugged on Lance's arm.

"It's probably best not to talk about business at a reunion," he said, stepping back from the table.

"Christine's not coming to the reunion because of the way you and Dee treated her," she said, ignoring Lance's caution.

"That's not right, Rebecca," countered Lance.

Kimberly tugged harder on his arm.

He looked in her direction as if to say *Wait a minute. I'm not finished.* Then he said to Rebecca, "It's true. Christine won't be coming to any of the reunion events. But not because of me … or Dee Evans …" Lance let his point hang while he waited for a response.

"Then why not? She and her husband were going to be sitting at our table. I've got you and Kimberly, Dee and Rhett Craddock, the Duncan's and Charles and me at the same table tomorrow night. If she's not coming, I'll need to find another couple."

"You better do that, because Christine Duncan won't be at the class dinner. They found her in the office this morning."

"They what?" she asked, a confused look on her face.

Lance took a deep breath and hesitated before answering. "She's dead, Rebecca. I don't have any details of how she died, but the fact is, Christine Duncan is dead."

"I knew she was distraught after she met with you, but … oh, my God. This is terrible."

With Kimberly by his side, Lance backed away. "Yes, it's terrible and certain to put a damper on things. By the way, Dee won't be at the FAC tonight either, but he said he'll attend the dinner tomorrow night. At least that's what he told me. You should probably give him a call to confirm."

"Oh, no," Rebecca moaned. "Christine Duncan's dead … what a way to begin our class reunion!"

CHAPTER SEVENTEEN

The expansive brick patio surrounding the Gazebo Bar was a perfect setting for mixing and mingling and unwinding from a week of work. Or tailgating before a CU football game. Or reliving memories of years ago with friends who had not seen each other in decades.

A grove of mature elm trees provided nice shade during the summer and early fall. Each tree was centered in a square planter box about ten feet on a side, the redwood beams also suitable for seating.

For additional protection from the Colorado sun, and also for insurance in the event of an untimely afternoon shower, the hotel had constructed a maze of gazebos that covered a generous area of the patio. The remaining open space contained an array of patio tables and chairs, some with umbrellas and some without. There was sufficient seating for the weary and plenty of room for people to stand around in groups large or small. There was also plenty of alcohol and enough food to satisfy most everyone's taste.

Lance had decided to change into khaki trousers and a colorful golf shirt that highlighted a flat stomach and thirty-four-inch waistline – not a bad physique for someone pushing fifty. Kimberly covered her petite body with a stylish summer dress accessorized with a pearl necklace and matching earrings. While they stood in the shade surveying the crowd, a short, compact man approached Lance from behind and whacked him on the shoulder so hard he momentarily lost his balance. "Lance Carpenter … old rifle arm … how the hell are you, ole buddy?"

"Well I'll be damned. If it isn't my favorite wide receiver. Best hands and quickest feet in the state."

"I don't know about that, Sir Lancelot, but we weren't too bad, were we?"

"Kim, meet Rhett Craddock. He's the one you spotted in the yearbook."

Rhett's eyes started on her face, then scanned down to her shoes and slowly back up, admiring every inch of her yellow linen dress as if he were the designer and she the model. With a disarming smile he said, "Very nice, Lance. You certainly have good taste."

Kimberly blushed at the exchange and held her hand out expecting Rhett to reciprocate.

"I don't take handshakes from good looking women," he said, brushing her hand to the side. "I only take hugs." Brashly he wrapped his arms around her, and Kimberly responded with a half-hearted embrace. He was only a few inches taller than she, so he bent forward for their cheeks to touch.

They separated awkwardly, and she finally spoke, "I usually don't accept hugs from a total stranger, but if you're one of my husband's high school buddies, I guess it's okay."

"I hope so. I certainly didn't mean to offend you. It's really nice to meet you … Kimberly?"

She answered with a nod and slight smile.

"And to see this guy?" Rhett continued, "Man, I'm telling ya … you look great. Must be that water you're drinking. You wanna belly up to the old Gazebo Bar and grab a brewski? Like the good old days?"

"Why not? Isn't that what reunions are for?"

"Damn right. I wasn't even going to come until I heard you were coming back to Boulder. Then I said to myself, 'What the hell, if Lance Carpenter's going to be there, then I'll be there, too. Might even be able to meet the lady who anchored him on the East Coast.'" Rhett smiled at the couple, and with a pronounced sweep of his arm, much like a maître'd at a fine restaurant, he led the way to the Gazebo Bar.

They ordered drinks. In less than a minute, the bartender set three bottles of Coors beer on the counter. Rhett grabbed two of them and left one for Lance. They found seats at one of the tables with an umbrella, and the guys stood shoulder to shoulder, waiting for Kimberly to sit down. Lance was a good six inches taller than Rhett, even with Rhett wearing a pair of Justin cowboy boots.

When Kimberly settled in her seat, Rhett slid a bottle of Coors in front of her and said, "You don't look like a beer gal. I would have guessed a glass of fine wine or some sophisticated drink, like a Martini or a Manhattan."

"Looks are deceiving, aren't they? I thought if I'm going to be with a couple of beer drinking buddies, why not join them." Kimberly held her long-neck bottle at arm's length.

The two men leaned forward and clinked their bottles against hers. "Cheers," they echoed. Everyone swallowed a first mouthful of beer, and then sat down side by side with Kimberly sitting across the table from Rhett.

Rhett looked comfortable in boots and jeans and a tight-fitting shirt that accentuated an athletic torso. His arms were tanned and toned, an indication of many hours in the sun and the gym, or an occupation that required physical activity outside. If he had not shaved his head, he would be completely bald on top with dark hair on the sides and back, an image suggested by a shiny forehead with a heavy shadow where sideburns and hair would grow.

Lance started the conversation. "You look great, Rhett. Where are you these days? I heard you stayed here in Boulder."

"You heard right. I'm still here." Rhett tipped the bottle back and swallowed a couple of mouthfuls of beer. "I'm a cop," he said proudly. "Actually, I'm a Deputy Police Chief with the Boulder P.D."

"Well how about that. Congratulations. Looks like you've stayed in great shape. You pumping iron or something?"

"Three or four times a week. I've got to stay up with the younger guys on the force. You know, set the example. I also run a few miles every morning. Before the sun comes up. Even when it's nasty cold outside."

"Good for you, Rhett. I wish I could say the same, but I'm lucky to workout once or twice a week, and sometimes I'll go a couple of weeks with no workout."

"Bad on ya, Lancelot. But you must be doing something right. You still look like you could suit up and play ... and fire that ball downfield to your favorite target."

"Yeah, right. If I tried that, I wouldn't be able to lift my arm for a week."

"Oh, come on, I know you're better than that. Are we ready for another round?"

Lance flashed a thumbs up.

Kimberly placed her palm on top of the bottle saying, "Not for me. I'm a one beer date." She had been sitting quietly, listening to former teammates talk about their high school days and how they got to where they are now. They had both summarized thirty years in four or five sentences. Kimberly had not said a word. When Rhett returned with two more beers, she asked, "Are you married? Have a family?"

"Not now," he said abruptly. "I was married once to a girl I met at CSU. Fortunately, we never had any kids. We only lasted a couple of years, and that was enough married life for me. How 'bout you? Do you have kids?"

Kimberly responded with motherly pride, "Yes, we have two daughters, both attending Boston University. One is a junior and the other a freshman. And now we're empty nesters, so I've started back to work."

"Really? He can't support you with kids in college?" Rhett grinned and sucked another mouthful of beer.

"Right, that's why I'm a working woman now," she said, tongue-in-cheek.

Rhett nodded approvingly, then said to Lance, "I knew you'd find someone perfect for you. This girl's got her act together."

Before Lance could respond, Kimberly continued, her eyes centered on Rhett's. "By the way," she said, "you said you weren't going to be at the reunion until you heard Lance was going to be here. How did you find out Lance would be coming back for the reunion?"

The question caught him by surprise, but it was innocent enough. *What does it matter*, he wondered, because he knew the answer would open a whole new topic of conversation.

His eyes narrowed, and Kimberly could tell cerebral wheels were spinning behind them.

Then he took a sip from the bottle, set it down on the table and sat back in the chair.

"Christine Duncan told me a few days ago." He waited for a reaction and then continued, "They found her body at 6:15 a.m. this morning. They also found a note she had written before she blew her brains out. The last sentence said, *If anyone cares why I did this, ask Lance Carpenter!* Your name was printed in capital letters and underlined three times. So, Lance, why did Christine Duncan put a bullet through her head?"

"Is this conversation part of an investigation?"

Rhett reached for his beer and swallowed another mouthful. "No, Sir Lancelot, that will come later. I just want to know, as your buddy, as your favorite wide receiver, what in the world did you say to Christine that would cause her to take her life?"

Lance gathered his thoughts before he responded. He glanced at Kimberly and then said, "That, as your teammate and someone you haven't seen for thirty years, is none of your business. If the jurisdictional authority wants to question me regarding my meeting with Christine Duncan, I'll be happy to accommodate. But with all due respect for your position as Boulder's Deputy Police Chief, I don't think it's appropriate for me to comment on Christine's death. It's sad and tragic, and it's likely to put a real damper on our reunion."

"Fair enough, Lance. We'll let it go at that. Are you up for another Coors?"

"No, thanks. I've had enough. Kimberly, how about you?"

"None for me. Remember? I'm a one beer woman."

Rhett pushed his chair back and rose to his feet. "Okay, then I'll see you tomorrow night. They've got us seated at the same table."

"That's what I heard."

"I want to hear more about your life in the big city," Rhett said, his eyes scanning the people gathered at the Gazebo Bar. "And it was very nice to meet you, Mrs. Carpenter," he said with feigned formality and a warm smile.

Kimberly extended her hand and responded in kind, "Nice to meet you, Chief Craddock. See you tomorrow night."

Rhett had been surveying the patio as he prepared to depart the Carpenter's company. "Look at this crowd. There must be a hundred people here. I'm going to mix and mingle and see who made it back for the reunion. Hey, there's someone I've been looking for. I'll see you guys later."

Like a man on a mission, Rhett Craddock headed straight for an attractive woman wearing a tight top and a short skirt. She was surrounded by three men, and they were all laughing as if someone had told a belly-buster joke, or recalled a funny incident from their high school days. From their actions, it was clear they had all had plenty to drink.

When Rhett joined the group, he and the woman met face to face a few feet apart. It only took a moment for recognition to sink in, and when it did, Rhett wrapped both arms around the woman and lifted her off the ground. He had found the "someone" he had been looking for.

Lance and Kimberly watched the affectionate greeting from their vantage point.

"Do you know those people?" she asked with a genuine curiosity.

"Oh, I know them all right. The three guys were all on the football team, and the woman is Jessica Malone."

"Do you want to say hello to them?"

"No, I'm sure we'll see them all tomorrow. I'm ready for some quiet time."

CHAPTER EIGHTEEN

～

The news of Christine Duncan's death began to spread among the people milling around the Gazebo Bar. Reactions were varied. Some folks were shocked, others sad. However, for graduates attending their thirtieth class reunion, the news of the death of a classmate was simply a reminder that life can be chock full of challenges and surprises; that with all the tough times and heartbreak that people face, it is important to count blessings and find some enjoyment every day. Seeing friends from a long time ago and hearing about the successes – and even the tragedies – in their lives, and finding out what everyone has done since graduation from dear old Boulder High School were the primary reasons for attending the reunion.

Long after the crowd had thinned out, a handful of Panthers gravitated to the smoking lounge off the lobby of the Millennium Hotel. It was reserved for special occasions.

Tastefully decorated with overstuffed leather chairs, dark wood tables and crystal ashtrays, the ambiance of the room suggested a place where a small group of businessmen could celebrate the closing of a huge real estate development deal. Or where a team of attorneys could gather to debrief the outcome of a litigation trial. Or where a few high school classmates could talk about things past.

Suzanne Johnson had reserved the room for the reunion and assumed responsibility for opening and closing the smoking lounge, as well as serving alcohol to the guests. Her liability was spelled out in a written contract she had signed with the hotel. Her guests included Rhett Craddock and Jessica Malone and three of Rhett's teammates.

A number of premium bottles of liquor were locked in cabinets behind the bar. Suzanne had the key. She had displayed two boxes of cigars on the bar. One was filled with ten *Cohibas* from *La Republica Dominicana,* and the other contained Churchill *en Tubos* by *Romeo y Julieta*, also from the Dominican Republic. The cigars were gratis. The guests would have to pay for the alcohol.

Everyone except Suzanne chose a cigar and lit up. She needed both hands to line up six shot glasses and fill them with premium Patrón tequila.

Rhett and Jessica were first to grab a shooter. The three other men followed suit. With a smoking cigar in one hand and a tequila shooter in the other, they all waited for Suzanne to catch up with them. They puffed away and watched as she removed a Churchill from an aluminum tube and handled it with the skill of an aficionado.

Suzanne rolled the cigar gently in her fingers and nodded approvingly. It was perfect. She ceremoniously slipped the capped end into her mouth and sensuously continued to roll the cigar.

Jessica rotated her cigar with her lips wrapped around it. She sucked a mouthful of smoke and blew it toward the ceiling.

The men cheered and grunted their approval of the two women engaged in a ritual that had historically been dominated by men.

With the cigar in one hand and a single blade guillotine held in the other, Suzanne snipped the cap of the cone. Then she put the cigar back into her mouth, flipped the top of a butane lighter and ignited the flame. She held the flame steady while she rotated the cigar and puffed and blew until bright red coals confirmed it was lit.

Then Suzanne Johnson abandoned her role as host and bartender. She grabbed the remaining shot of tequila from the bar and joined the others in a tight circle in the middle of the smoking lounge. "A toast," she said triumphantly as she raised her shot glass for the others to clink. "To the good old days and a great reunion!"

"I'll drink to that."

One of the guys chimed in, "I'll drink to anything."

"I'll drink to rekindling old flames," Jessica said, her slurred words suggesting she already had too much to drink.

With that, six shot glasses met so convincingly that precious tequila spilled over the brims.

"Cheers," they said in unison.

"To good times and good friends. I can handle another shooter."

"Me, too."

Rather than speaking, Jessica puffed and held a mouthful of smoke. She pursued her lips and positioned her tongue while the others watched. Then she raised her chin and tipped her head back slightly. Her mouth opened slowly, and with the precision of an expert, three perfect circles of smoke drifted upward. "I'll have one more," she said.

"Way to go, Jessie."

"The bottle's on the bar. You can help yourself," Suzanne said, her role as bartender over.

Jessica reached for the Patrón and filled her glass again. "Anyone else want another shooter?"

"Not me," Rhett said. "One's my limit."

Suzanne and the other three guys held their empty shots at arm's length while Jessica poured another round.

"You always could hold your liquor better than anyone," Rhett said as he curled his arm around her waist and gently pulled her to his side.

Jessica dipped her eyes to the floor and then looked up at Rhett. "Better than you, that's for sure." Her dark brown eyes focused on Rhett's. She raised her glass to her lower lip, and with one quick flip of the wrist, she belted another shooter.

Rhett tightened his hold on Jessica's waist and drew her closer. Their lips met and opened. He tasted the tequila on her tongue.

For some reason – perhaps in deference to the others in the smoking lounge – the passionate kiss ended as quickly as it had begun.

"Do you remember the last time we did this?" Rhett whispered.

"Did what?"

"Drank shooters."

"How could I forget?"

One of Rhett's teammates overheard the conversation and said, "After the last game."

"Yeah, how could we forget *that* night. We went down in flames. You dropped *two* touchdown passes."

"Carpenter threw *three* interceptions," Rhett quickly added.

"I saw you talking with him earlier tonight. How's he doing?"

"He's doing great. He's some big financial executive in Boston. All settled down. A family guy."

"He sure bombed in football at Boston College."

"The beginning of the end was our last game in the state playoffs. I don't think he ever recovered from that."

"Someone keyed his pickup at the party at his friend's house."

"I don't remember that."

Jessica chimed in, "Yeah, *someone* slashed a big 'L' on the driver's side door. And it didn't stand for Lance."

"Too many shooters. The night got out of control."

"Tequila always wins," Jessica grinned.

"So does weed," one of the guys added. He reached into his pocket and in a cupped hand, he showed a small bag tied with a string.

Suzanne immediately stepped in saying, "Not in here, you idiot. I'm responsible, and we've got the Deputy Police Chief here for crying out loud."

"Yeah, I should bust you for possession."

"Go ahead, Crado. I dare ya."

"Don't tempt me, Tate. Or I just might throw your gay ass in jail."

"Okay, that's enough," Suzanne intervened. "I'm closing this place down before things get out of hand. Besides, we have the tour of the high school at nine o'clock tomorrow morning. Are you guys going?"

"Are you kidding me? I had enough of BHS to last a lifetime," one of them said while the others nodded.

"Me, too," Jessica added with a chuckle as she tapped the lit end of her cigar in an ashtray. When it was out, she set it down and said, "At nine o'clock I'll still be in bed."

Rhett smiled at the thought. "Me, too. It's the weekend. I always sleep in on Saturday and Sunday. Unless there's a good reason to be awake."

Suzanne looked disappointed. "So none of you will make the tour? I hope we'll see you at Stadium Club for the dinner-dance."

"I don't dance, but I'll be there."

"We'll all be there," Rhett said. "Unless these guys break the law and get thrown in my jail."

"Oh, come on, Crado. You wouldn't do that to your old buddies, would you?"

Rhett Craddock did not answer. Instead, he turned to Jessica, reached for her hand and spoke quietly, "Let's get out of here."

She squeezed his hand. Together they left the smoking lounge and walked across the Millennium's lobby to the elevator, leaving Suzanne and Rhett's teammates alone to talk about the good old times.

CHAPTER NINETEEN

≈

In Jessica's room on the third floor, Rhett pressed her against the wall using the full force of his body while they kissed passionately with open mouths.

They clawed at each other's clothes and threw pieces of clothing on the carpet as they stumbled to the bed.

When they were finished, Rhett rolled to his back and stared at the ceiling. Jessica curled up beside him, their bodies still wet and warm. With her left arm draped over his chest, Jessica closed her eyes.

Rhett remained still while her breathing slowed and soft, purr-like sounds emanated from deep in her throat. He thought about the first time they had made love the night the Panthers lost in the state playoffs.

Jessica Malone had been one of Lance Carpenter's girlfriends during their senior year. They had dated, but their relationship had remained platonic, and Jessica wanted more. She dumped him after the last regular season game, and they did not speak until the party following the big defeat in the state playoffs.

Lance was devastated by throwing three interceptions and losing the game; Jessica was drunk and throwing down tequila shooters as if they were lemonade. Their argument led to pushing and shoving and words that shocked even the crudest attendees.

It was Rhett Craddock who stepped between them to calm everyone down. It was Rhett Craddock who took Jessica Malone home. It was the first time that Rhett and Jessica had been together.

She awoke when Rhett got up to go to the bathroom. When he returned bedside, she asked, "Do you remember the last time we did this?"

"Did what?"

"Drank shooters."

"How could I forget," Rhett replied as he slid back under the covers. He propped a couple of pillows against the wall and found a comfortable position beside her. "It was you, wasn't it?"

"It was me who what?"

Rhett smiled and continued, "It was you who keyed Carpenter's pickup."

"I don't remember anything that night."

"You obviously remember making love with me."

"Oh, that," she said, sliding one arm under the pillows and resting the other one across his chest. "Yes, I sorta remember *that*." She snuggled closer and placed her head on his shoulder. "But I want to know why it's been thirty years between screws. It was so good that first time. I wanted more."

Rhett squirmed a bit. "It didn't work out, you know, with the football season coming to an end. You being Carpenter's ex, and me getting into basketball. I mean, it just didn't work out."

"What about the camping trip at Eldorado Canyon? We could have been together that night. I was alone in my tent."

"That was a terrible night. We should have come home when it first started raining, but Coach MacAdams decided to stay, a decision that cost him his life."

Jessica removed her arm from Rhett's chest and sat up beside him. She pulled the sheet up and tucked it under her arms to cover her breasts. "MacAdams was drinking beer and smoking a joint," she said. "I can remember that night like it was yesterday."

Long after midnight, Jack MacAdams sat quietly on a log beside a smoldering campfire in Eldorado Canyon. An unexpected rain had shortened the evening and all the kids from the Boulder High School Climbing and Hiking Club had returned to their tents more than an hour before.

Alone, and now regretting his decision to remain in the canyon overnight, MacAdams had drained a couple of cans of Coors Light and fired up a joint. The distinctive smell of marijuana wafted from the campsite as Jessica approached. MacAdams heard her coming and turned to see who was there.

Jessica wore black sweatpants and a long sleeved COLORADO sweat shirt. Her hair was pulled back and tied in a pony tail with a yellow band. As she approached MacAdams, the light of a half moon shone on her face.

"Jessica? You should be asleep by now."

"I can't sleep."

"Why not?"

"The ground is hard and I hear sounds."

"Sounds?"

"Yeah. Weird sounds. Like crickets, or twigs breaking under footsteps. It's creepy, and I'm freaked out."

MacAdams remained seated on the log and hid the joint behind his leg. "Who's in your tent?"

"No one. I can hear people snoring in another tent. They talked for hours," she whined. Jessica looked down at the smoking campfire and continued, "How about putting some more wood on the fire?"

"No, Jessica. The fire's almost out and you need to get back to your tent."

"I'm wide awake, and I don't want to be in my tent alone. And I don't want to be standing here while you're doing pot. Are you going to share it, or not?"

Realizing he had been caught, MacAdams stood up and slowly raised the joint to his lips. A bright red glow illuminated by his fingertips as he inhaled. "No, Miss Malone, I am not going to smoke pot with one of my students. And you are going to keep your mouth shut about this."

"Oh, come on. Everyone else is down for the count. I won't tell if you don't tell." Jessica stepped closer. "I don't have anything on under these sweats," she said.

With that, MacAdams tossed the joint on the glowing embers and watched it burn. "You need to come to your senses, Jessica. I'm not going to let you get us both into trouble."

"Oh yeah," she said provocatively. "You call this trouble?" She reached for the bottom of her sweatshirt and raised it to show her bare breasts.

"That does it! You've crossed the line!" He tossed the beer can in the fire and started toward her.

Jessica pulled the sweatshirt over her head and held it with one hand behind her back.

"Put that back on," he ordered.

Her breasts were completely exposed, full and firm, the nipples popped out from the cool mountain air. "No, I want you to see them. Touch them."

MacAdams tried to reason with her. "Now look, this isn't going to happen. You put that sweatshirt back on and get back to your tent. If you do, none of this happened. Understand? If you don't, then I'll have to report you for inappropriate conduct."

"And I'll report you for drinking beer and smoking pot with your students!"

"That's not true."

"That's what I'll tell everyone."

MacAdams swayed as he stepped closer to her. Then he stopped, steadied himself and began to speak.

Suddenly she lunged forward and wrapped both arms around him, still holding the sweatshirt in one hand. She pressed her bare breasts against his chest and tried to kiss his lips.

MacAdams turned his head away and tried to break free without hurting her, because physically, he could easily overpower her.

She aggressively kissed his neck and tried to lick his ear. Finally, he broke away and pushed her back forcefully.

"Now stop it," he said quietly, hoping to end the encounter without waking others. "Jessica, this has gone way too far. You're an attractive young woman. You're one of my students. Not only **can't** we … I do not want you!"

The words cut deep. She was young and vulnerable and half-naked, and the hurtful expression on her face prompted an explanation.

With compassion and resignation, Jack MacAdams said, "Jessica, it's not you. It's me."

"What do you mean by that?"

"Just what I said. I do not want you. I don't want women … period!"

Jessica stepped back as she digested his words.

"I'm gay, Jessica. I thought everyone knew that by now."

Jessica's eyes flared. She threw her sweatshirt at his face and rushed toward him.

His reaction dulled by the combination of beer and marijuana, MacAdams lost his balance and tripped over the log he had been sitting on earlier. As Jessica's flailing body collided with him, MacAdams held on while they spun to the ground.

Out of control from the momentum of the fall, MacAdams landed on his back with Jessica's full weight on top of him.

She heard a sickening thud, the sound of his skull crashing against a boulder; he cried out in pain, and then his arms went limp and fell to the ground.

Jessica rolled off him and kneeled by his side. She used both hands to pull her sweatshirt from underneath his body, causing it to shift on the ground. Even in the darkness of the night, Jessica could see that his eyes were fixed upward in their sockets. She saw blood oozing from a deep gash in his head.

Frantically she thrust her arms into the sleeves of her sweatshirt and then pulled it over her head. It was wet and cold.

She backed away from MacAdams.

He moved and groaned. He tried to sit up and then crumbled back to the ground.

As she thought about the night in Eldorado Canyon, Jessica nestled closer to Rhett. "You could've had me if you wanted."

"I know."

"Really?"

"Sure, you made it pretty obvious."

"You remember that night, too?"

"Don't we all?" Rhett repositioned the pillows under his head. Then with his fingers, he moved a lock of jet black hair that had covered her cheek. "I'll remember tonight, too."

Jessica forced her leg between his. "Are you going to stay with me tonight, or are you going to be one of those guys who packs up and leaves?"

Rhett chuckled. "Well, let's see. This is a Friday night and I like to sleep in on the weekend."

"Good," she said as their bodies closed together. "Then we can make up for lost time!"

*   *   *

When Jessica awoke, she was alone in bed. "Rhett?" She called his name and heard no response.

She rolled to the side of the bed. Still naked with her head pounding from too much tequila, the dominant thoughts in her mind were last night's sex and Rhett's promise to sleep in on a Saturday morning. If he had slipped out without so much as saying goodnight, she was going to be pissed.

Jessica closed her eyes and massaged her temples with the palms of her hands. She felt as if her head was about to explode.

Slowly she stood up beside the bed, steadying herself with her arms extended to each side, as if they were wings of an airplane. The room swirled around her, and she felt the rumble in her stomach. With considerable experience in situations like this, Jessica knew her options. She could kneel by the toilet and wait for the inevitable upchuck, or she could sprawl back on the bed and hope to feel better with a few more hours of sleep.

"Rhett?" His name hung in the air. She waited to hear his voice.

You bastard, she thought as her head hit the pillow. Jessica pulled the blanket over her shoulder and in a few minutes she was sound asleep.

CHAPTER TWENTY

In Boulder, most Saturdays in August provide opportunities for outside activities like biking, mowing the lawn, going to the grocery store or simply hanging out with a newspaper and a cup of coffee at the nearest Starbucks. But for people attending a high school reunion, it was all about getting caught up and celebrating being together again. The venue or activity didn't matter. They were curious to see who had changed the most, who looked good and who had gained the most weight, and they were most interested in hearing about one another's lives since graduation. That had begun on Friday night and would continue for the duration of the reunion.

Rebecca Carlin arrived at the main entrance to Boulder High School a few minutes before nine o'clock. As she approached the building, she looked at two relief figures above the door, affectionately known as Minnie and Jake. Recalling the tradition of hazing night for new sophomore women, she bowed to the concrete statues.

The door opened and a man wearing faded jeans and a purple T-shirt greeted her, "Good morning, Rebecca."

"Hey, Eric. Are we ready for the tour?"

"All set. How was the FAC?"

"It was great. We missed you."

"I know. I was interviewing candidates for a manager's position at the library."

"On a Friday night?"

"Uh huh, it was a scheduling problem. We had three people on campus and it took all day long. We're going to make an offer next week."

Eric Bartholomew had been the editor of the student newspaper, *The Owl*, during their senior year. Now an associate director at the CU Library, Eric had been a key player on Rebecca's reunion planning team and had agreed to lead the tour of the high school. It was also his task to collect all the photos that were sent in by classmates planning to attend the reunion. Using technology at the library, Eric had located hundreds of old photos from their high school days. He had personally paid for 150 copies of a sixteen page mini-*Odaroloc* that he had created especially for the reunion.

Rebecca and Eric entered the main lobby of the school to wait for their classmates. A security guard sat in a chair behind a table inside the door, positioned to screen and assist visitors during normal school hours.

"Would you like to see the brochure, hot off the press?" Eric had brought two copies of his masterpiece with him. The guard was looking at one of them, and Eric handed the other to Rebecca. "The cover turned out great."

"Wow!" she exclaimed. "This is marvelous, Eric."

"Thanks. I'll have them at the Stadium Club tonight. We can give one per graduate, and if anyone wants extra copies, they can buy them for ten dollars each."

"How much did these cost you to produce?"

"You don't want to know."

Rebecca shook her head as she began to flip through the pages. "Wow," she said again. "This is great. They're going to love it."

She continued scanning the photos and reading captions until something grabbed her attention. She held a page open. There were four photographs on the page, two in black and white and two in color, the before-and-now photos of a guy and gal.

On the bottom half of the page was the black and white photo of the guy with a full head of wavy dark hair with a shadow covering one eye, and the colored photo showed a shaved head and piercing blue eyes. The caption read *Rhett Craddock, changed the most.*

On the top half of the page were the pictures of the girl. Her senior picture was on the left and the smaller of the two. The colored photo was taken at a portrait studio, and it showed the same pretty face, peaceful smile and warm, seductive eyes as the photo that had been used for the yearbook thirty years ago. The caption read *Christine Tanner Duncan, changed the least.*

Rebecca froze and asked, "Eric, have you heard about Christine?"

"No, but I love those pictures. Do you like the way I morphed the senior pictures into their latest photograph?"

"Yes, that's very nice. But Christine … she's dead. She committed suicide yesterday."

Eric's eyes widened. "Oh, my goodness. Do people know?"

"Some do, but not everyone."

"Well at least everyone will have a nice picture to remember her by." *Suicide?* thought Eric, shaking his head in wonderment.

While they waited in the main lobby for their classmates to arrive, Rebecca wondered how to inform people of Christine's death. Should they make an announcement or let the news spread by word of mouth? Eric thought about the same thing, and he decided how best to handle a very difficult situation.

"We'll start the tour in the courtyard," he said. "If you'll meet people here and let them know we'll be meeting in the courtyard, I'll take it from there."

"Sounds good to me," Rebecca said as she continued to turn the pages of Eric's brochure.

With the punctuality of students attending class, all of the people who wanted to go on the tour of dear old Boulder High showed up a few minutes before nine o'clock.

Eric met them in the courtyard, an architectural square of textured concrete slabs flanked on three sides by classrooms and offices. The main school building was three stories, and the walkways framing the courtyard were guarded by steel railings. Two massive sets of stairs provided access to all three levels of classrooms as well as a clear view of people gathered in the courtyard.

When he was ready to begin the tour, he walked up to the first tier landing of the east staircase and asked for everyone's attention. More than forty people had signed up for the tour. They wore comfortable and casual clothes, shorts, tennis shoes and T-shirts. Some brought their children along. Catch-up conversations were interrupted when Eric began talking.

"Good morning, everyone. Welcome back to Boulder High School. I am Eric Bartholomew and I recognize many of you, but to make it easier for all of us, please wear your nametags. Most of us have not changed much in thirty years, but a lot of you have brought guests—wives or husbands or significant others—and we want to know who belongs with whom. For the dinner at the Stadium Club tonight, all the BHS graduates will have a nametag with their senior picture on it."

Eric looked down from the staircase and scanned the crowd. For the most part, everyone looked up and listened. Some of the attendees were more interested in each other and continued talking among themselves. One couple held hands and peered through the windows of the library. The children looked bored.

Eric held a copy of his brochure above the railing and continued talking. "You'll also get a copy of this tonight." He showed the cover and then opened the brochure to the centerfold, holding it open with both hands above his head and moving so everyone in the courtyard could see it. "I think you'll like this because it contains many pictures you've never seen before. Anyway, you'll get these tonight."

He closed the brochure. His smile disappeared. "Now before we start the tour, there's some bad news. Some of you may have already heard, but Christine Tanner died yesterday. She was planning to be here with us and she sent me her portrait for the book. I hope that's the way we will all remember her."

From the reaction to the announcement, Eric and Rebecca knew that Christine's death was a shock to most. The news created a buzz around the courtyard.

"She committed suicide," one of the women told another.

Larry Tate, a lanky, balding man wearing a polo shirt with a pair of sunglasses dangling in front said, "I heard it was because of a meeting she had with Lance Carpenter. He's a VP in the same company, and the word is, he fired her."

"Carpenter? Is he here?"

"I haven't seen him, but I heard he's back for the reunion."

"Is he still in Boston?"

"Yeah, I think so, but I'm not sure. I heard he came back because Dexter Evans is getting some big award."

"They were best friends. I could never figure that one out."

"I still can't," Tate continued.

"It'll be good to see Lance Carpenter. He should be *here*." He pointed to the floor of the courtyard for emphasis.

"Huh?"

"Right *here*! This is where he and MacAdams duked it out. Remember?"

"Do I remember? I was right in the middle of it. It was the Monday after we got knocked out of the state playoffs. A bunch of us football players were hanging out in the courtyard when Carpenter comes up and apologizes for having a bad game. He was pretty bummed about the loss, but to top it all off, someone keyed his pickup at the party after the game, and you could tell he was still hurting inside. That's when Coach MacAdams walked by."

"I'm sorry, guys. You can blame me for the loss. I never should have thrown that pass. Crado was covered, but I thought if I could lead him enough, he could get to it. I never saw the safety."

"*I was breaking free and I thought it was going to be a touchdown,*" Rhett Craddock added, defending his quarterback.

"*I dropped two passes in the second half. One of them would have been for a first down. Instead we had to punt,*" Larry Tate said.

"*Yeah, it was a team loss, Lance. Not your fault. We let you down. We had a chance to go all the way this year and now it's over, but there's no sense beating ourselves up over it. We need to move on.*"

Lance listened to his teammates talk. His head was down, shoulders drooped, the pain from a devastating loss still very much weighing on his mind. "But if I had not thrown that pass, we could have pulled it out."

Coach MacAdams overheard the conversation as he made his way through the courtyard to the gymnasium. "If … if … if," he said, his words dripping with sarcasm. He stopped a few feet away from Lance and said, "If you had listened to your coaches … if you had executed your reads … if you kept your mind on football instead of all the other distractions around here, we'd be playing next Friday night. That's the bottom line." He turned away and started walking in the direction of the gym.

Lance felt the pain again. He dropped his books to the courtyard floor. All except one. He gripped his math book by the binder, and with all the force he could generate in his powerful right arm, he hurled it at the back of MacAdams' head.

Fortunately for the coach, the book opened and the pages fluttered in the air as the book sailed past his head and landed harmlessly at the feet of another group of students.

MacAdams stood frozen in the courtyard, trying to decide whether to ignore the incident or reprimand Lance Carpenter on the spot.

But for Lance, no decision was necessary. The emotions inside erupted like an angry volcano. He pushed Rhett aside and boldly walked toward MacAdams, who had anchored a position in the center of the courtyard.

Lance stopped face to face with his coach. Their chests touched. Their arms dangled by their sides with fists clenched.

"*You're a son-of-a-bitch,*" *Lance said through his teeth.*

"*You're a loser, Carpenter.*"

Lance's teammates had followed him, urging him to calm down. Other students had heard the yelling and turned their attention to the confrontation between coach and player. Everyone gravitated around them to hear and take sides.

When Lance drew his fist back, Tate grabbed his arm and tried to constrain him.

Rhett rushed at MacAdams and wrapped his arms around him to prevent any blows from landing. They spun to the ground, and Rhett lost his grip.

MacAdams swung at Craddock.

Carpenter elbowed Tate and leaped on MacAdams.

And then the brawl began.

"It was never the same after that."

"Yeah, Carpenter got suspended from school for a week."

"I got fifteen stitches here." Larry Tate pointed to a scar half hidden by a bushy eyebrow highlighted by wild gray hairs.

"And MacAdams got in trouble big time with the administration. The fight ended his career as a coach."

"I heard it was something else," the tall, balding man said as he removed the sunglasses from the front of his polo shirt and put them on.

"You sure have *heard* a lot of stuff."

"People talk. I listen."

Before his classmate could respond, Larry Tate turned his attention to Eric Bartholomew, who had been talking about the historical significance of the courtyard at Boulder High School. It was the place where people hung out during the school day and the place where graduates made the Senior Throw. Beginning in elementary school, they had saved papers and class notes for the purpose of hurling them over third floor railings knowing that underclassmen would clean the courtyard the next day.

It was the place where the life of Jack MacAdams had begun to unravel.

CHAPTER TWENTY ONE

~

After a full day of doing whatever they wanted to do in Boulder, graduates of the Class of 1978 and their guests were ready for the capstone event of the reunion. Rebecca had polled everyone for preferences on venue for the class banquet, and the top choice by a wide margin was the stadium at Folsom Field. Overlooking the football field, the university and downtown Boulder, the Byron R. White Club provided the perfect atmosphere for mixing and mingling, recollection and reflection.

Dee Evans was deep in reflection as he walked along the cavernous pedestrian malls beneath the press box of the stadium, where thousands of people gathered on a handful of Saturday afternoons each fall. However, on this particular day, there were no long lines at the serving windows of the Boulder Pizza Company, and only about one hundred people were expected for dinner and dancing at the Stadium Club.

Four enormous black and gold Colorado Buffalo pennants hung from the steel girders high above the walkway. Dee saw a group of four or five people ahead of him, but he did not recognize any of them. When he got to the elevators to the club level, the people were gone. He pushed the UP button and waited for the next elevator. A moment later, the door opened and Dee stepped inside.

"Hold the elevator," a voice thundered from the hallway.

Dee stuck his foot between the doors as they closed, and automatically they retracted open. He pressed the button that held the doors open and waited for others to join him.

"Thank you," the man said, hurrying to the elevator while his companion followed a few steps behind.

When she was safely inside the elevator, Dee released the button and the doors closed. "Going up?" Dee asked lightheartedly, racking his brain for the name of the woman. For the second time, he punched the button for the club level and the doors closed.

"You're Dexter Evans, aren't you," she said.

"Yes, and you are ..."

"Jan Fuller, and this is my husband, Tom Ferguson. He went to Fairview."

"Nice to see you both," Dee said politely. "Do you still live around here?"

"Uh huh. We've got a home in Arapahoe, and our business is in Denver. How 'bout you?"

"I spend most of my time in San Jose, but I still have a home in Boulder."

"The one on Knollwood?"

"That's the one," Dee responded as the elevator stopped and the doors opened. He held his right hand against the bumper, and with a sweep of the other one, he waited for the couple to exit.

"Congratulations on your award," the woman said as she stepped out of the elevator. "You've done well for yourself."

"Thank you, Jan," Dee responded coolly, almost as if he were embarrassed by the recognition. "It's good to see you again."

His words lacked sincerity even though that was not what he intended. Dee Evans had never been comfortable in the spotlight, and he was not interested in getting caught up with classmates or meeting their spouses. He had avoided the Friday night reception and the tour of the high school. The banquet would be the only reunion event he would attend. His plan was to stay close to Lance and Kimberly Carpenter, accept his recognition as the distinguished graduate, and get the hell out of there. At least, that was his plan.

"There he is now," Rebecca said when she saw Dee and the other couple approaching the welcome table.

Three persons sat behind a table covered and skirted with black fabric. The young man in the middle was flanked by two young women wearing stylish black dresses, one sleeveless showcasing well-toned, suntanned arms, and the other with spaghetti straps that revealed the outline of a swimsuit top. All three were smiling broadly when Rebecca greeted Dee with an embrace. "This is my son, Andrew," she said, introducing Dee to the young man behind the table. "And his friend, Lisa. They're both graduates of Boulder High School. Class of 2005."

Dee reached out and shook their hands, and Lisa handed Dee his nametag.

Turning to the young woman on the right, Rebecca continued the introductions. "Dee, this is Sally Verona's sister, Valerie. She was our photographer at the reception and the tour of the high school. It's too bad you missed those events. They were a lot of fun."

"I remember Sally," Dee said, ignoring Rebecca's needle. "But I'm sorry, I didn't know she had a younger sister."

"We're seven years apart, but we're still very close. She's right over there."

Dee looked where she was pointing. A group of three women stood with their backs to the windows overlooking an empty football stadium. They were posing and smiling broadly for another classmate with a disposable camera from one of the tables in the room.

Dee immediately recognized Sally Verona, the one in the middle. She was the tallest of the three, striking with her summer tan and shoulder-length blonde hair beautifully pulled back to show her full face and pleasant smile. She wore a black floral print dress with bouquets of red roses tastefully arranged from the wide shoulder straps to the hem of the dress. Dee did not recognize the other two women.

"Your sister hasn't changed a bit," Dee said to the young lady at the welcome table.

"I know. She always looks great."

"Looks like it runs in the family," he added, his smile accenting the compliment.

She accepted it with grace and said, "I hope you enjoy the evening."

As Dee turned away from the table, Rebecca cocked her head toward the sea of round banquet tables set with white tablecloths, purple napkins and a basic selection of glasses and white dinnerware. The centerpiece for each table included helium-filled, purple and gold balloons anchored by purple and gold ribbons, some straight and others curled to add a touch of whimsy.

The room was filled by the time Dee arrived. Many people were already seated around the banquet tables waiting for dinner to be served. Others huddled in groups of three and four, wine glasses filled, conversations in full swing. A few couples sat on tall bar stools by counters conveniently installed around pillars in the room. Also mounted on the pillars and throughout the room were television monitors used primarily for replays during CU games or other contests of interest.

Tonight, however, the monitors showed a continuous loop slide presentation prepared by Eric Bartholomew. The collection of old photographs he had found, and the new ones sent in specifically for the reunion, added a nice touch for the evening – a blend of the past with the present and a stimulus for conversation, even though that was not necessary.

"Our table's over here," Rebecca said as she led Dee to a table near the dance floor where Lance and Kimberly Carpenter were already seated. Rhett Craddock was there, too, talking with Rebecca's husband, who was not a graduate of Boulder High School.

Lance's appearance reflected his role as an East Coast financial executive—black sport coat, light gray dress slacks, white shirt with a handsome, black and silver Neiman Marcus tie, a gift from Kimberly on his forty-ninth birthday. Kimberly was a picture of understated elegance in a beautiful black sheath dress that she wore with strappy heels and a simple pair of diamond earrings. They both had their nametags prominently displayed.

"Hello again, Dee," Lance said when they got to the table. Their hands clasped together, and Lance noted the firmness in Dee's grip.

"I spoke to JP last night," Dee said, his eyes telegraphing a sense of satisfaction and expectation. "It's a done deal. He's authorized you to sign the documents. He FedEx'd them to me today. Did he call you?"

Surprised, Lance said, "We talked yesterday, but he didn't say anything about signing a contract."

"He said he would be speaking with you personally."

"Let's see, it's eight o'clock in Boston. I can give him a call."

"Go ahead. Call JP. Because when this thing is over tonight, I'd like you to come to the house and sign the papers. I've got an early flight from DIA to San Jose tomorrow morning, and I want to seal the deal and move on."

The ladies overheard the exchange. Kimberly knew what they were talking about; Rebecca did not have a clue. When she sensed their brief conversation was over, Rebecca introduced Dee to her husband, Charles, who had been engaged in a conversation with Rhett Craddock. They had stood when the ladies approached the table and were waiting politely for everyone to sit down.

Dee circled the table to shake hands with the two men, and then, with a gentlemanly gesture, he helped the ladies take their seats.

Lance reached for his Blackberry and held it where everyone could see it. "Excuse me. Business calls." He walked away from the table looking for a quiet place to call JP Tompkins in Boston.

A few minutes later, Lance returned to the table where everyone was still engaged in pleasant conversation. "You're right, Dee. It's a done deal. We can sign the papers tonight."

"Terrific. It's been a long time coming."

Rhett listened and then interrupted, "What is this, you guys? A business meeting or our class reunion?"

Dee sat back triumphantly and declared, "It's actually both. We're all here, seeing each other for the first time in thirty years—and later tonight, Lance and I will be completing a negotiation that has been years in the making. I'm taking my company public, and the Diversified Global Investment Bank, with Lance Carpenter the responsible executive, will be handling everything."

"Wow, that's impressive," Charles muttered.

"Yeah, I'm impressed," Rhett added. "Sir Lancelot rides again. And who would have ever believed Dexter Evans would be the distinguished graduate of our class? Congratulations to both of you."

Dee smiled but said nothing.

"How about a toast to our distinguished graduate?" Lance raised his glass and waited for the others to join him.

"To Dee," one of them said.

"To the DG."

"To Rebecca for pulling us all together," Lance added.

"To meeting new people," Rhett said as he tipped his glass toward Kimberly's.

"I'll drink to all of that," Rebecca's husband concluded. "*Salute!*"

With that, everyone drained their drink, refilled their glass and waited for dinner to be served. It was the beginning of what promised to be an interesting evening of conversation and celebration, remembering and reflecting.

CHAPTER TWENTY TWO

≈

T he slide show of pictures from high school days, interspersed with more current photos of members of the Class of 1978, looped into its fifth cycle. Most everyone had seen every photo at least a couple of times, except Dee Evans, who was one of the last to arrive at the Stadium Club.

From his seat at the table near the risers where the dance band was set up, Dee had a close-up view of a television monitor. Between bites of mixed green salad and sips of wine, he saw the latest portrait photograph of Christine Duncan fade to a grainy snapshot of Lance Carpenter standing tall in the pocket, his arm cocked, and two tacklers wrapped around his waist. A series of senior pictures from the *Odaroloc*, each followed by the more recent photo of the person, captured Dee's attention.

When Laurence Tate's photos showed on the screens, Dee scanned the room looking for him, knowing that his physical appearance had changed dramatically in the past thirty years. From a scrawny lad with a head of shoulder-length, wavy brown hair to a tall, balding man with a thirty-four-inch waist, Larry Tate had been one of the first to sign up for the reunion.

He sat at the table nearest the bar on the north side of the room, with a line-of-sight view of the main table where Dee was seated. He happened to be looking at Dee when their eyes met and locked. He waved his hand and telegraphed his delight.

Dee answered with a single nod, then looked back at the television monitor just as Larry Tate's photograph disappeared. It was followed by another snapshot that showed Tate with a group of classmates piling out of a van at a campsite in the Colorado Rockies.

Dee knew the photo was taken by Jack MacAdams the day he took the climbing club to Eldorado Canyon, the day Coach Mac plunged to his death. The memory was still very fresh in his mind.

At another table in the center of the room, Jessica saw the climbing club photo. "That was the worst night of my life," she said to no one in particular.

"What was?"

"That." She pointed to the television monitor. "Our climbing club trip."

"When the coach cashed it in?"

"Uh huh."

"It shook up the school, but I don't think people were all that upset. He was kind of a jerk, wasn't he?"

"I know he didn't get along with everyone. Remember when the big brawl erupted in the courtyard? I thought Carpenter was going to strangle him until Larry Tate and Rhett Craddock joined the fight."

"They were with you on the climbing club trip, weren't they?"

"Who?" Jessica looked back at the monitor and the photo of MacAdams' climbing club had been replaced by a snapshot of Panther cheerleaders posing for the camera with their heads together, big smiles, and pompoms massed in front.

"The jocks—Carpenter, Craddock and Tate."

"Are you kidding me? Carpenter and the coach never spoke after the fight. Rhett and Larry were on the trip. So were Rebecca, Sally Verona and Suzanne Johnson. There were six of us plus Coach Mac. Four girls, two guys and Jack MacAdams. It turned into a disaster when it started raining. We should've headed back home, but the guys thought the rain would stop. It turned out to be the worst night of our lives."

"Especially for Jack MacAdams."

With conversations in full swing at every table in the room and staff nearly finished serving desserts, Rebecca decided it was time to make a few remarks to the class and their guests—and to make the distinguished graduate presentation to Dee. She folded her napkin and placed it beside her plate. She leaned over to kiss Charles on the cheek and whispered, "Here we go, my last official duty of the evening."

"Then we can dance. Right?"

"Whenever you're ready."

Rebecca Carlin had worked hard to pull the reunion together. She handled most of the communication electronically and spent an inordinate amount of time sending email reminders, answering every message and trying to contact more people. She also talked on the telephone with people who planned to attend as well as those who were reluctant to return. With about 570 people in the class, Rebecca was elated with a turnout of more than 200 for the welcome reception on Friday night and the dinner dance on Saturday. Based on all she had heard, everyone was having a great time, and she looked forward to having it all behind her.

The musicians of the Painted Pony dance band sat patiently at the bar, waiting for their cue to begin playing. Their instruments were arranged on a rectangular platform about eighteen inches high, tucked against the east wall with black drapes providing an elegant backdrop for the program and the band.

Having already consumed two glasses of wine, Rebecca carefully stepped up the two-stair riser at the north end of the platform. She walked to the microphone stand centered on the parquet dance floor, and with a sense of satisfaction, watched the animated conversations in progress. Before she began to speak, someone at a table near the dance floor tapped a spoon on a glass to get everyone's attention.

"Thank you," Rebecca said, acknowledging the gesture. "Thank you, everyone."

A few more people tapped on their glasses and beer bottles, but still the buzz of conversation filled the room.

Rebecca stood at the microphone holding her notes in one hand and waving at the crowd with the other. "Hello out there. Helloooow. Thank you, everyone."

Finally people realized that Rebecca was standing at the microphone, so they turned in their seats and waited for her to continue.

From his chair, Eric pointed a remote at the DVD player sitting on a portable cabinet beside the platform, and the television monitors darkened.

"Good evening, Class of 1978. Did you enjoy the slide show?" Rebecca asked rhetorically. "Let's hear it for Eric Bartholomew for all the work he did with the slide show … and for the brochure you got tonight … and for organizing the tour at the high school. Stand up, Eric. Great job.

"Our program tonight will be very short, because I know you want to spend most of your time getting caught up with classmates. I just want to thank everyone for coming, including people from Fairview, our spouses, guests, everyone. Thanks for being here."

Rebecca referred to her notes and then looked over at the bar. "Before I introduce our distinguished graduate, I want to thank the Painted Pony for playing tonight. They're great and you're really going to enjoy them.

"I also want to thank Suzanne Johnson, Sally Verona and her sister, Valerie, and my son, Andrew, for all their help with the planning details. To borrow a line from the Academy awards, without them, I wouldn't be standing here tonight.

"I said the program will be very short, and that's a promise. So now, it's my pleasure to introduce Dexter 'Dee' Evans, who is Boulder High School's Distinguished Citizen of the Year for 2008. As everyone in this room knows, he was the smartest guy in our class … and the word on the street is that stock in his company will soon be traded on the NASDAQ. How about that? Perhaps we can get him to offer classmates a few shares at bargain rates. Is that legal, Dee?"

Spontaneous applause signaled approval of Rebecca's suggestion.

She smiled at Dee and said, "Ladies and gentlemen, our distinguished graduate, Dee Evans."

Rebecca waited for Dee on the bandstand.

Lance and Kimberly stood when he left his seat and proceeded up the two-stair riser to the microphone. By the time he and Rebecca embraced, almost everyone in the room was standing, clapping with appreciation for Dee's recognition as one of their high school's most successful graduates.

He waited for Rebecca to get back to the table and for everyone to take their seats. With all eyes focused on him, Dee Evans looked around the room. He recognized many of the faces staring at him, but some of the people in the room were complete strangers. He smiled at the Carpenters, Rhett Craddock and the others at the table where he had been sitting. He saw Larry Tate beaming back at him. He saw Jessica Malone leaning close to Sally Verona, speaking with her lips only inches from Sally's ear.

Dee swallowed to clear his throat, and then he began. "Thank you for the short introduction, Rebecca. As we agreed, I'll also keep my remarks very brief, because all these people came to our thirtieth reunion to get caught up with each other, not to listen to speeches or relive the past.

"Of course I am honored to be recognized as a distinguished graduate of our high school, and I thank you all for the warm reception tonight. Maybe there *is* a way to create a Boulder block of stock for classmates who want to invest in Evans Software Solutions. I'll leave that to my good friend, Lance Carpenter, who will be handling the initial public offering. We hope to have everything in place by the end of the year.

"I've been very fortunate to be in the right place at the right time since we graduated from dear old Boulder High School. I had some great professors at Stanford. I went to work for a great company in Palo Alto. Then one day an idea popped into my head and I started thinking about open-source database software applications that could be used to improve Web-based technology. And the rest is history.

"From the class geek to the CEO of a half billion dollar corporation, it's been quite a journey. But the entrepreneurial challenges of starting your own business – and building it from a staff of three with limited resources to a company with more than 300 employees and annual revenues exceeding two hundred million – pale in significance to the challenges faced by a gay man living in a straight world."

Dee Evans paused to let his words sink in. He had lived a tortured life, at first confused by his own feelings, and ultimately certain of his sexuality. He had kept the secret hidden during his high school days, college years and throughout his professional life. And now, with one simple sentence, he had opened the door for new challenges.

Dee scanned the room for reaction to his revelation.

Lance and Kimberly exchanged looks and turned their attention back to Dee. Rebecca appeared ambivalent, her husband dumfounded. Rhett stared at the center of the table.

Across the room, Larry Tate pushed back in his chair, folded his arms across his chest and sat silently, waiting for Dee to continue.

Sally Verona turned to Jessica and said, "I don't believe what I just heard."

"I do."

"He was kind of a nerd, but I never thought he might be gay."

"Well, now you know."

Sally mused and said, "How about that? Our distinguished graduate is a gay millionaire!"

After the noticeable pause, Dee picked up where he had left off. "When I was a little boy, I dreamed about being an astronaut like Neil Armstrong. In high school, I just wanted to be popular, like Eric Bartholomew, Rhett Craddock and Larry Tate. But as many of you know, my time at Boulder High School was painfully difficult for me."

Dee's voice cracked with emotion. With the knuckle of his right hand, he wiped a tear from the corner of his eye.

So did Tate and his partner.

"But you should know that I owe much of my success in business to another member of our class, someone I admire greatly and hold in the very highest regard to this day. That someone is Lance Carpenter."

Dee looked at Lance and pointed directly at him. "Lance, you were the star athlete, the guy everyone wanted to be like. I was a nobody. The guy everybody shunned. And you stuck by me, made me feel important. If it had not been for your friendship during high school, I would have given up right then and there. So thank you from the bottom of my heart, my friend, and thanks for being here tonight."

Lance nodded to show his appreciation.

Kimberly wrapped her arm around his back and squeezed with affection.

A few others began applauding while Dee stood smiling at the microphone with an air of confidence, a renewed sense of self worth, the poise of the chief executive officer of a half billion dollar corporation.

He reached into his coat pocket and withdrew a small metal object.

"This may surprise some people here tonight, but I think it's time for me to return this to the rightful owner." Dee held up a class ring with two fingers so that everyone could see it. "This is *your* ring, Lance. It's been tucked away in my jewelry box for thirty years now. Come to think about it, I've kept many things hidden way too long, and I feel a great sense of relief to have them out in the open.

"I thank you for honoring me as one of the distinguished graduates of Boulder High School, but most importantly, I thank you for giving me the opportunity to share the burdens of my soul. Please accept my best wishes for every success in your professional and personal lives."

For the final time, Dee surveyed the audience. As he turned to leave the stage, most of the people stood and clapped; others remained seated with folded arms.

Rebecca pushed her chair back and met Dee at the bottom of the steps. "We sure didn't expect that," she said to him in passing.

"I know, but it had to come out some day, and I thought, why not tonight? I'm among friends. Right?"

Rebecca had no words for response, so she stepped to the microphone for her closing remarks. "Wow," she began. "That took some courage, but he's among friends. Right? Let's have one more round of applause for Dee Evans—and a warm welcome for the Painted Pony band."

Rebecca waved the musicians to the stage and continued, "Thank you all for being here tonight. The band will play 'till the last couple leaves, so enjoy the rest of the evening."

When Dee returned to the table, Lance was the first one to meet him. Their handshake turned to a hug, and they stood face to face. "Here, this is yours," Dee said, holding the ring in his palm.

Lance smiled as he took it and said, "I'm sure there's a story behind this."

"Only that it's been weighing me down for thirty years, and giving it back to you gets the elephant off my back. You'll be coming over tonight, right?"

"Right. We're going to stay for a few dances, and I'll be at your house before, let's say, eleven thirty."

"Good. See you later."

By the time Rebecca returned to the table, Dee had abruptly departed the Stadium Club, giving no time for further interface with any of his classmates.

But his comments had ignited a firestorm of reaction that would burn well beyond the last dance.

CHAPTER TWENTY THREE

~

While watching a dozen couples dancing on the small parquet floor, the person sitting next to Larry Tate leaned closer. "Is Lance Carpenter gay?"

"I don't think so. I mean, look there. It sure looks like he's a happily married man to me."

"Bummer. He would have been a great partner."

"Better than me?"

"No one could be better than you. Would you like to dance?"

Tate reached under the table and placed his hand on his partner's knee. "I don't think that's a good idea. It would totally freak these people out."

"You're right. We can have another drink and then meet at Bentley's Bar. After all, it's Saturday night and the night is young."

Tate tapped his agreement on the knee, then dragged his fingers over the leg as he brought his hand back into view. He folded both hands together and rested them on the table in front of him.

"Can you believe it? We thought twice about coming to this reunion together, and the frigging star of the night makes this his coming out party. You gotta be kidding me."

"I always wondered about him," Tate said.

"Really?"

"Uh huh. It goes back to high school. He knew I was, but him?

I wondered, but nothing ever came of it." After a few moments of thought, he continued, "The ring thing? How do you suppose Dee Evans got Lance Carpenter's class ring?"

"I don't know. That's why I asked the question. Is Carpenter one of us?"

"Well, there's your answer."

Larry Tate and his partner watched as Lance and Kimberly held each other closely, dancing to Billboard's number one tune of 1978, Rod Stewart's hit "Tonight's The Night."

They danced cheek to cheek, their bodies moving together in perfect harmony. Lance smiled as Kimberly sang along softly with the lead singer of the band:

> *Tonight's the night,*
> *It's gonna be all right,*
> *Cause I love you girl,*
> *Ain't nobody gonna stop us now.*

"Isn't love grand?"

Larry Tate's eyes locked with his partner's. "Yes, it is. Ain't nobody gonna stop us now!"

* * *

With Jessica standing by his side, Rhett leaned on the railing of an outdoor balcony on the east side of the Stadium Club. The balcony overlooked a soccer field three stories below them. Lights from the city and the university campus sparkled in the darkness of the night. A few blocks away, Rhett could see the grounds of the Millennium Hotel, where he and Jessica had been the night before. They could barely hear the loud music playing inside.

"You're deep in thought," Jessica said as she nudged closer. "Are you thinking about last night?"

"No, I'm thinking about tonight." Rhett turned to her and wrapped his arms around her. He pulled her tightly against his body, and instantly their mouths opened and their lips pressed together.

Jessica gave him a few seconds of passion, and then she pulled away. "You lied, you bastard. You left me all alone."

"You were zonked out, Jess. I stayed 'till morning, but it looked like you needed a few more hours of sleep. So I went out for coffee."

"And you didn't come back! What I needed was you by my side."

Rhett smiled and said, "I'm by your side now. Would you like to dance?"

"Sure, and then I'd like an encore performance, this time with no tequila."

"Ah, bummer, tequila makes your clothes fall off."

"I don't need tequila for that." Jessica's eyes twinkled as she lifted her chin and waited for a kiss.

Rhett leaned forward and softly kissed her lips. No passion, no tongues thrashing, just a single kiss. "So would you like to dance?"

Jessica took his hand and led him to the balcony door. When he opened it for her, the music grew louder, and they could hear people singing: *Rolling, rolling, rolling on the river.*

"Are you up for that?" she asked.

"I'd rather wait for a slow one. Besides, I need to ask Rebecca about Lance's ring. Didn't she have it on the climbing club trip to Eldorado Canyon?"

"Probably, but I didn't see it. After we broke up, I couldn't care less about his stupid ring, but it pissed me off that he gave it to *her*."

"I didn't think you were the jealous type."

"It wasn't jealousy. It was hate!"

"As I remember, you were a bit out of control back then."

"What makes you think I'm not out of control now?"

Rhett let the question slide for a few seconds. He spotted Rebecca talking with Sally Verona. Her husband sat alone at the table looking bored. "I think I saw the ring, but the question is, how in the world did it wind up in Dee Evans' jewelry box?"

"Who cares?"

"I'm not sure," Rhett replied. "But I'm certain Lance Carpenter and Rebecca Carlin want to know."

*   *   *

When "Proud Mary" was over, Lance and Kimberly returned to the table and sat down. Lance wiped his brow with a handkerchief while Kimberly drank the remainder of her ice water.

Dee had already gone home. Eric had migrated to another group of friends leaving Rhett at the table with Rebecca and her husband.

"You guys have all the moves," Rhett said to the Carpenters, who were still recovering from ten minutes of rocking and rolling on the river.

"I'm out of shape."

"I'm out of breath," Kimberly added.

"It's the altitude. Remember, you're in the mountains."

"I know. I like your mountains, but I love the Atlantic Ocean."

"Never seen it. In fact, I've never been east of Omaha."

"You should come for a visit some time," Kimberly offered. "Come in the fall when the leaves are turning. It's the most beautiful time of the year. If you plan it right, you could go to a BC game with us."

"That would bring back a lot of memories," Rhett said.

Rebecca's husband chimed into the conversation. "You're right. The colors that time of the year are fantastic, just like when the Aspens turn gold here in Colorado. Except you've got miles and miles of reds and oranges and yellows and golds—absolutely breathtaking scenery along the highways. We were in DC for a conference in October a few years ago, and we stayed afterward for fifteen days. We rented a car and drove from DC to Camden, Maine, with a couple of days in Newport, Rhode Island, and Boston. It was a memorable vacation."

"Hey, I'm from Camden. That's where Lance and I were married."

Lance quickly added, "You were in Boston and didn't give us a call?"

Rebecca responded, "I didn't know you were in Boston, and even if I had known, I doubt we would have called. Our split was pretty ugly if you remember."

"Oh, I remember, but that's all behind us now. Is it too late to say I'm sorry?"

"It's never too late to say I'm sorry."

With all the sincerity he could muster, Lance said, "Then I'm sorry, Rebecca, and now that you know we're in Boston, let us know the next time you venture east, and we'll show you the sights."

Rhett sat quietly listening to the chit chat. He wanted to know about the ring. "So you guys have finally made up after all these years?"

"I think it's time we move on. Don't you?" Lance waited for Rebecca's answer.

"I guess so," she said reluctantly.

"You're not so sure?"

"Some things are never forgotten."

Sensing Rebecca's uncertainty and the residual emotion of a distant relationship, Kimberly interjected, "But everything can be forgiven."

"Very well said," Rebecca's husband added.

"And tonight you got your ring back." Rhett looked at Lance for a reaction.

"That was a surprise to me."

"Me, too," Rebecca admitted.

"You told me you threw it over a cliff in Eldorado Canyon."

"Well. That wasn't exactly true. I lost it on the camping trip, and I just wanted you to think I threw it away. You hurt me and I wanted to hurt you back."

"It worked," Lance said resignedly. "But as the love of my life just said, everything can be forgiven."

"You lost the ring on the camping trip?" Rhett asked quizzically.

"Uh huh."

"Then I wonder how Dee Evans got it."

"I don't know. You'll have to ask him."

"I will, but first I promised Jessica I'd dance a slow one with her."

For the next hour, the band played slow tunes, some people danced, and others remained at their tables sharing tales of the past and plans for the future. Eventually, the reunion attendees began leaving in small groups. For most of them, handshakes and hugs marked the end of the evening and the beginning of anticipation for the next class reunion.

Rhett and Jessica had other plans.

Lance had to sign a contract at Dee's place, because Dee was leaving for Denver International Airport first thing in the morning, and the Carpenters would be flying back to Boston on the corporate jet before noon.

Rebecca and her husband were the last couple to depart the Stadium Club on Saturday night, leaving the life-sized bronze sculpture of Byron "Whizzer" White overlooking the darkness of Folsom Field.

CHAPTER TWENTY FOUR

≈

D ee had been home alone for about thirty minutes when he heard the garage door open. He had changed from his suit and tie into baggy sweat pants, a black tee shirt and a pair of leather moccasins. The documents, FedEx'd directly to his home from Boston by JP Tompkins, were stacked on the corner of his desk, ready for signature. Dee expected Lance within the hour, although they had not set a specific time for signing. He grabbed the papers and started downstairs to meet Jeffrey and prepare for Lance Carpenter's visit.

At the bottom of the stairs, Dee saw Jeffrey coming from the garage. "You're home early for a Saturday night."

"It was an awful night. After the movie, I stopped by Bentley's, and I saw Greg with another guy. He told me he was going to Colorado Springs to see his mother. I just sat in the corner and watched them—and then they left together. I am so devastated."

"Did they see you?"

"I don't think so."

"Then don't worry. He'll be back, and you can talk about it. Until you know what's really going on, there's no sense worrying about it."

"But I can't do that. I'm so upset my stomach is nauseous. How can I not worry?" Jeffrey stood by the doorway to another set of stairs leading down to his living area in the Knollwood home. He slumped his shoulders and stared at the floor, a pathetic picture of a desolate young man.

Holding the stack of documents in one hand, Dee wrapped his free arm around Jeffrey's shoulder, and with a gentle tug, pulled him to his side. "You'll be all right, Jeffrey. I'm certain you'll be all right. And you may be interested in what happened at the dinner tonight."

"You got your big award."

"Yes, but I surprised everyone by what I said during my acceptance remarks." Dee removed his arm from Jeffrey's shoulder and they stood facing each other. "I let the whole world know I'm gay."

Jeffrey straightened and stepped back. "No, you didn't. Did you really?"

"Yes, I did, and I feel great."

"I didn't think you would ever do that."

"Neither did I. But after hearing about Christine Duncan committing suicide, and seeing my old buddy, Lance Carpenter, I decided it was time to get everything out in the open. You know, Jeffrey, I've been living with secrets my whole life, but you? You've been willing to be out, and willing to be authentic in living your life from an early age, something I never felt I was able to do. Your presence in my home has been good for me, and I'm very grateful to you for what you've done. Tonight I decided to free my own soul … to let people know who I really am. So it's done, and my new life is just beginning. Who knows where it might lead."

During the two years that Jeffrey had lived in Dee's home on Knollwood, their relationship had remained that of landlord/tenant with an occasional conversation more like that of a father and son. Though Dee knew Jeffrey was gay when he agreed to let him live in his home, he never acknowledged his own sexual orientation, nor had there been any physical expressions of affection between them. So when Jeffrey sprung forward and threw his arms around Dee, they were both surprised.

Dee accidentally dropped the documents. Gently he held the young man and patted his back to comfort him. "Everything will be okay, Jeffrey," he said, shifting the focus back to Jeffrey's heartbreak. "You'll pull yourself together and be a stronger person. If you and Greg are meant to be together, you'll work it out. If not, it's not the end of the world."

When they parted from the hug, Jeffrey nodded in agreement. He turned away to hide the tears that had welled in his eyes.

Dee looked at the papers scattered on the floor. "Lance Carpenter will be here in a few minutes to sign these documents," he said. "Could you brew a pot of coffee for us?"

"Okay," Jeffrey responded meekly.

"Do we still have some of those wonderful chocolate chip cookies you made?"

"Uh huh."

"Very good. A pot of coffee and a plate of cookies. We'll be in the fireplace room. You can leave the goodies on the dining room table."

"Okay … and by the way, Dexter, thanks for your fatherly guidance and support. I needed that."

"You're going to be okay," Dee repeated with a warm smile.

Having regained his composure, Jeffrey went to the kitchen to brew the coffee.

Dee kneeled down and began collecting the papers strewn about the parquet floor. Fortunately, each page was numbered, and within a few minutes Dee had them reassembled and placed side by side on the coffee table, ready for signature.

He climbed back up the stairs to his office off the master bedroom, where he would read emails and make one telephone call while waiting for Lance to arrive.

Dee noted the lower right corner of his computer screen. *10:58 p.m.* He had thirty-two minutes to wait.

* * *

Lance and Kimberly held hands as they walked down the hallway to their corner suite at the St. Julien.

"My feet are killing me," she said.

"That's the most we've danced in years."

"It sure beat sitting around talking about your high school glory days."

"It wasn't that bad after all, was it?"

"No, actually, I quite enjoyed meeting some of your friends. Rebecca's as nice as she can be, and Dee, he's really an interesting guy. Did you know he was gay?"

They reached their suite and Lance slipped the key card into the door. He studied her face and said, "Not in my wildest dreams. He was on the eccentric side, but I never thought anything of it. We grew up together, hung out and went to parties together. Stuff like that. That's about it."

Lance led the way into the room and headed straight for the closet. He slipped his sport coat from his shoulders and hung it with his other clothes, all ready for packing for the flight back home to Boston in the morning.

Kimberly kicked out of her shoes, sat down on the side of the bed, crossed her right leg at a right angle and began massaging her foot with both hands.

"I wish I didn't have to meet Dee tonight. I'd much rather stay here with you. I could give you a nice foot rub."

"What time do you have to be at Dee's?" she asked.

"I told him I'd be there before eleven thirty."

"Then you better go now. I'll rub my own feet."

Lance took off his tie and rolled his shirt cuffs to mid-forearm while he talked, "I don't think I'll be gone long. We'll sign the contract, say our goodbyes, and I'll be back before midnight."

Kimberly had reversed her leg cross and busily she kneaded the arch of her other foot with the knuckles of a fist. "Try not to wake me when you get back. I'm really tired."

"Then I'll kiss you goodnight right now," he said, bending down to reach her lips. "Sleep tight, sweetheart. I love you."

"Love you, too."

With that, Lance left the room and headed for the lobby of the hotel. He had asked the night bellman to bring the Escalade from valet parking to the front entrance, and both were waiting for him when he came through the double glass doors. Lance handed the bellman a ten dollar bill, settled behind the steering wheel, and ten minutes later, he parked in front of the wood-paneled garage doors at Dee's home.

Lance felt different this time. Two hours ago his best friend from high school announced to the class that he was a gay man. *For how long?* he wondered. *How was it that I never detected Dee's sexual orientation?*

Sure, Lance knew Dee was not interested in girls like Rebecca or Jessica, or for that matter, any of the young ladies at school. Most everyone assumed he was most interested in astronomy, physics and understanding how gadgets work, and that's why he made little effort to get along with girls.

But knowing changes everything.

Yes, Dee had become a successful entrepreneur, built a multi-hundred million dollar enterprise, and made it clear to JP Tompkins that he wanted Lance to handle the initial public offering on the NASDAQ. They had been best friends in high school. However, Lance now knew Dee Evans was gay, and that grated against every moral fiber in his body.

Emotionally scarred by his childhood experiences with Father John and the encounters with Jack MacAdams, Lance had become homophobic, to say the least. He could not envision two men having sex together without becoming extremely uncomfortable, which is how he felt as he sat in the Escalade anticipating a late night meeting with an openly gay man. *How in the hell is this going to go?* he wondered as he glanced at the digital clock on the panel in front of him. *11:12 p.m.* It was time for him to find out.

CHAPTER TWENTY FIVE

〜

S lowly, a 2008 Tahoe turned into an empty parking lot at the Centennial Trailhead, one of the open space and mountain parks maintained by the City of Boulder. Its tires crunched the gravel surface as the car stopped.

The driver turned off the headlights and sat quietly, his heart pounding. He waited for a few moments, then took a deep breath and opened the car door. He left the key in the ignition and felt for the handgun he had placed on the passenger seat. When his eyes adjusted to the darkness of the night, a two percent illumination on the twenty-eighth day of the moon's cycle, he started up the wooded hillside that towered in back of Dee's home.

From the parking lot, he straddled the lower railing of a split-rail fence and climbed about one hundred yards of steep grade covered with pine trees and scrub oak. When he reached the top of the hill, he stopped to catch his breath and survey the route he would have to take to remain unseen. He saw lights from the kitchen through a wall of floor to ceiling picture windows. Drapes were open and lights were also on in the upstairs master bedroom.

Carefully he started down through the waist-high mounds of wild grass dominating the hillside, looking for the rock stairs that he knew were there. Halfway down the hillside, a mule deer darted from the grassy area into the trees. He froze, and from that vantage point he saw someone in the kitchen.

With a short distance to go, he moved more quickly down the rock pathway to a thicket of blue spruce trees near a corner of the deck. He crouched behind an aluminum barbeque grill a few feet from the kitchen door and observed the young man preparing a tray with coffee cups and a platter of cookies. On the television in front of him, Mariska Hargitay studied a body lying beside a dumpster in a grungy New York City alley.

He waited and watched.

He saw Jeffrey standing behind a granite-topped island in the kitchen, facing the windows along the back side of the house. Near the island a few feet from the back door, he noticed a small, white desk cluttered with a laptop computer, a printer, two wire baskets stacked and filled with papers, plus a few books pushed to the edge of the desktop. Beside the desk was a tall bookcase that held not only cookbooks, but also family photographs and knick knacks.

Jeffrey fussed over the presentation on the tray. Meticulously, he rearranged his selection of chocolate chip cookies until they were just right. Finally, he centered a spoon over each napkin, and when finished, he stepped back and threw both hands in the air, admiring the work he had done.

From his hiding point behind the barbeque, the intruder watched Jeffrey scoop the tray up with both hands and leave the kitchen. Through the picture window in the dining room, he saw Jeffrey place the coffee and cookies on the dining room table, just as Dee had asked him to do. Then he returned to the kitchen, quickly tidied up the mess he had made, turned off the TV and in a flash retreated to the privacy of his living quarters downstairs.

The intruder waited patiently, making certain Jeffrey would not be returning to the kitchen. He tiptoed to the back door. To his surprise, it was unlocked, and he slipped inside the house. In a heartbeat, he hid behind the bookcase and waited for his next move.

With an ear cocked to the interior of the house, he listened intently.

He heard a voice above him talking on a telephone. *That must be Dee in his office upstairs,* he thought.

He heard the front doorbell ring.

He heard footsteps on the stairs getting louder with each step down.

A moment later he heard Dee greet someone at the door. He heard, "Come on in, Lance."

He did not see Dee's broad smile and open arms. Or the stoic look on Lance Carpenter's face.

He inched closer to the corner of the bookcase and continued to listen.

"Sorry I didn't stick around to talk after dinner," he heard Dee say to Lance. "You know I've never been much of a socializer."

"I know, but I never really knew why. Until tonight."

Lance stepped inside the foyer and Dee closed the door behind him. "Let's sit over there," Dee pointed and led the way through the formal living room to the family room that he had recently redecorated with new paint and furniture. "You probably don't remember mom and dad's stuff in here, but I just couldn't keep it any longer. I don't use this space very often, but at least it looks updated in case I want to put this place on the market. And I just might do that."

Lance saw the papers spread out on the coffee table, and rather than commenting on Dee's refurnished family room, he said coldly, "You know, Dee, it's late, and we've got some business to take care of."

"We'll get to that, but first, how about some coffee and some homemade chocolate chip cookies?" Dee walked over to the dining room table, grabbed the tray Jeffrey had prepared, and carried it carefully back to the coffee table. He placed it right on top of the documents he and Lance were to sign. "They sure look good, don't they?"

"They do, and I'm vulnerable to homemade cookies. Did you paint the fireplace?" Lance asked, feigning interest.

"I didn't like the old bricks and the dark walnut bookcases, so I decided to paint everything white. I just love the way it turned out."

Still uncomfortable knowing he was in the home of an openly gay man – never mind that he had once been his best friend – Lance searched for something more to say. "I like the Oriental area rug. Where'd you get that?"

"Oh, thank you. I found it in a nice little store in La Jolla. Can't remember the name. When I saw it, I knew I just had to have it."

"The colors are perfect for this room."

"They should be. I pulled the mauve from here," Dee kneeled and pointed to a spot on the Oriental rug. "I think the wall color matches it perfectly."

"I didn't know you were interested in anything other than computer technology."

"You didn't know I was gay, either. Did you?" Dee sat down beside Lance on the sofa and reached for a cookie.

"Nope."

"Surprised?"

"To say the least."

"Is it going to make a difference in our relationship?"

"How can it not?"

"You'll just have to separate your feelings for me personally from the business at hand. And if you can't do that, then I'll have to find another firm to handle my initial public offering—and JP won't like that." Before Lance could respond, Dee continued, "I meant what I said tonight, Lance. You still mean the world to me. If it weren't for your friendship during high school, I would have killed myself. Seriously, you were the one responsible for helping me get through a very difficult time of my life."

Lance thought for a moment and then he said, "Fair enough, Dee. I'm ready for one of your homemade chocolate chip cookies."

"I didn't make them. Jeffrey did."

"They're tasty," Lance said as he swallowed the first bite, then washed it down with a sip of hot coffee.

For the next few minutes they talked and reminisced and munched on cookies. Lance had overcome his initial anxiety over Dee's coming out, and soon Dee was more like the Dee that Lance remembered.

Then the doorbell rang again.

CHAPTER TWENTY SIX

~

J essica Malone had been very troubled by the ring. If Dee Evans had found it, then he must have been at the campsite the night Jack MacAdams was killed. Had he seen her bare her breasts? Did he see her land on top of MacAdams as they spun to the ground? Did he hear the sickening sound of his head crashing against a boulder?

She had to know.

The questions had haunted her as she left the Stadium Club alone. Rather than returning to her room at the Millennium Hotel, Jessica pointed her car in the direction of Dee's house. She had been there with Lance a couple of times during high school, but he always drove. With her horrible sense of direction, she only vaguely knew where she was going.

As she wandered aimlessly around the tree-lined streets on Mapleton Hill she became more and more upset. The alcohol she had consumed at the Stadium Club did not help her navigate through neighborhoods where, by eleven o'clock at night, all the lights were out and the residents were sound asleep.

She became totally frustrated looking for Dee's house. Finally, Jessica recognized where she was. At the corner of Seventh Street, she turned right and slowly proceeded west on Mapleton until it became Sunshine Road. Now she focused on how she would confront Dee about the ring, and most worrisome, what she would have to do if he had seen everything at the campsite.

Deep in thought and feeling like her gut was lodged in her throat, Jessica missed the turn to Dee's house. *Damn it!* she thought as she drove along the narrow, unlit street crowded by overgrown trees and vegetation. She looked for a place to turn around.

On her left she saw a driveway. As she turned, the headlights lit a sign at the entrance to a parking lot. She stopped, shifted to reverse, and began backing out of the parking lot. When Jessica turned back east, her headlights shone on a single vehicle tucked along a split-rail fence at the far end of the parking lot.

She stared at the dark blue Tahoe.

Jessica's car blocked both lanes of Sunshine Road, so when she saw headlights approaching, she immediately pulled back into the parking lot. Rather than backing up, she inched forward through the empty lot, her attention glued on the Tahoe.

When the headlights beamed squarely on the SUV, her suspicions were confirmed. She had seen that Tahoe last night, parked in front of the Millennium Hotel, but it was not there when she left the hotel for her daily walk thirteen hours ago.

That bastard, she thought as she hurried out of the parking lot and turned right to Knollwood Drive. A minute later she stopped on the street in front of Dee's house. She grabbed her handbag and walked up the steep driveway.

When she passed the Escalade, she thought about the night she keyed Lance's pickup parked in the very same spot. She remembered the lower front door led to the downstairs recreation room where they had partied hard, where she had consumed far too many tequila shooters.

She knew her visit would catch Dee Evans by surprise, but she didn't care. She had to know what he saw at the campsite and how he got Lance's ring. She was the one surprised when Jeffrey, wearing pajamas and a silk robe, cracked open the door to see who had rung the bell. "Is Dee home?" she asked, her words and breath evidence of alcohol consumption.

"Is he expecting you?"

"No, but I want to see him. We didn't have a chance to talk at dinner tonight."

Jeffrey noted her evening dress and the small bag she clutched in her hand. "Who are you?" he asked, his body blocking entrance to the house.

"Jessica Malone."

"Dee's upstairs with Mr. Carpenter. It's a business meeting and I don't think they'll want to be disturbed." Jeffrey started to close the door.

Jessica stepped forward and stopped the door with her leg. "Wait. Just tell them Jessica's here. They'll see me."

When she removed her leg from between the door and the door jam, Jeffrey shut the door and turned the lock. A minute later she heard the lock unlatch and the door opened.

"They're upstairs in the fireplace room," Jeffrey said with no enthusiasm. "I'm going to bed."

Without answering, Jessica watched him circle in front of the built-in bar and disappear through a door off the recreation room. She could not remember a bedroom downstairs, but she certainly remembered the bar, the party and keying Lance Carpenter's pickup.

Her mind focused and her heart began beating faster as she started up the carpeted staircase.

She held the railing to steady her steps. When she looked up, she saw Dee waiting for her at the top of the stairs.

After a brief exchange, he led her back to the fireplace room where Lance waited.

"What a surprise to see you here," Jessica said, foregoing the pleasantries and getting right to the point. Her voice was strong, her words only slightly slurred.

"There have been many surprises tonight, wouldn't you say?" Lance sat back down and reached for his coffee cup. "Care for a cookie?"

Jessica scoffed at the offer. Instead she railed and squared off face to face with Dee. "No, I don't want a God-damned cookie! I want to know how you got his God-damned ring!" Her words boomed and bounced off the walls.

"Calm down, Jessica," Dee said quietly. "There's no need to be upset. I'll tell you how I got the ring ... and you won't be surprised."

"Where?" she snapped.

"When you settle down and act civil, I'll tell you. It looks like you've had too much to drink. Just like the last time you were in this house. Remember that night, Lance?"

"I think we all do," he said.

"Let me get you a cup of coffee, Jessica," Dee said stepping toward the pot on the tray.

"No, I don't want any coffee. I don't want anything! I just want to know where you got Lance's ring."

"Okay, Jessica, I'll tell you." Dee stood on the Oriental rug with his back to the fireplace.

Lance stayed seated on the sofa and waited to hear, because he wanted to know, too.

Jessica planted her feet shoulder-width as if she expected Dee's explanation to knock her for a loop.

"At the campsite. After everyone had returned to their tents," Dee said matter-of-factly.

"You weren't even there," she countered.

"Oh, yes I was."

Jessica's brow furrowed. Her eyes narrowed. "There were only two guys on the trip to Eldorado Canyon."

"That's right."

"Did you see MacAdams?"

"I did. He was drinking beer and smoking pot."

"Did you see me at the campsite?"

"Yes, I saw you, too." Dee looked straight into her bloodshot eyes and nodded. "Yes, Jessica, I saw everything. I saw you take off your sweatshirt. I saw you try to kiss him. I could see the two of you arguing, but I couldn't hear what you said. I was too far away."

"Did you see us fight?"

Dee nodded.

"Then you know what happened?"

"Yes, I do."

Jessica stepped back and teetered between Dee standing in the middle of the room and Lance sitting by the coffee table. She clutched her handbag in front of her.

"You lunged at him and the two of you spun to the ground. You landed on top and he didn't move. A minute later, I saw you running away. That's when I went to Jack. He was on his back. His eyes were closed. I saw blood coming from a terrible gash on the back of his head, and when I tried to stop the bleeding, he opened an eye."

Jessica and Lance listened intently. So did the person hiding behind the bookcase.

"Jack recognized me and touched my arm. Then his eye closed and his arm dropped to the ground. That's when I saw the ring. He had been holding it in a clutched fist."

"Then Rebecca had been there, too."

"She was the first one to come back after the rain stopped."

"Apparently she wanted a fling with MacAdams, too. He pushed her away, and in the struggle, the ring must've been ripped from a chain around her neck. I saw Jack pick something up after Rebecca left. It must've been Lance's ring."

"You gotta be kidding me," Lance said. "Both Rebecca and Jessica wanted a piece of MacAdams?"

It was more of an exclamation than a question, but Dee responded, "That's what it looked like to me."

Lance shook his head.

"What else?" Jessica demanded.

"He opened his eyes and mumbled something to me. I leaned closer to hear."

"And?"

"He asked me what I was doing at the campsite. I told him I wanted to know what he and Larry Tate were doing on the camping trip." Dee looked first at Jessica and then Lance. He waited for a reaction from either of them.

"I don't understand. You were there to see MacAdams and Tate? You suspected …" Lance stopped mid-sentence, searching for words.

"That they were *both* gay." Dee said. "I knew Larry was, and I heard what Jack did to you the week before the state playoff game. I never forgave him for that."

Lance stiffened.

"The son-of-bitch!" Jessica barked. "He told me he was gay that night. And I thought he was dead when I left him lying on the ground. For all these years I've believed it was me who killed Jack MacAdams, that he died as a result of our fight, and that he must have accidentally fallen over the ledge after he bashed his head on the boulder."

"No, Jessica, I can assure you he was very much alive when you left him. Very hurt and very high, but very much alive."

"I've carried guilt everywhere I've been for the last thirty years, and now you're telling me it was not my fault?"

"Yes—it was not your fault. I know that for a fact. When Jack and I were talking, I heard someone coming. I had to get out of there, so I went back to hide in the bushes. I know how MacAdams died. I know who killed him, and Jessica, it was not you."

The man hiding behind the bookcase had heard every word. "It was me," he announced as he stepped from his hiding place into the doorway.

All three turned and saw Rhett Craddock standing by the dining room table with one gun pointed at them and another weapon strapped to his side.

CHAPTER TWENTY SEVEN

~

R hett Craddock, Boulder's Deputy Chief of Police, slowly waved a 9mm Glock 19 pistol back and forth from Lance to Jessica to Dee. The silencer added another seven inches to the barrel. He sidestepped toward the fireplace, and with the business end of the Glock motioned for Dee to move closer to Jessica. When Lance started to stand up, Rhett ordered, "Don't move, Lancelot. It's too bad you got wrapped up in all of this."

"You son-of-a-bitch," Jessica screamed. "You told me he was dead!"

"He was *almost* dead, and he deserved to die, the queer bastard."

Dee winced at the word and inched closer to Jessica.

Lance considered leaping up and tackling Rhett, but with him pointing the Glock alternatively at him and Jessica and Dee, that was out of the question. Plus, Rhett had slowly worked his way to the fireplace and managed to narrow his field of fire.

Rhett had always known he might have to kill again. But he never thought he would have to kill a woman who had shared his bed. Or the guy who had thrown all the touchdown passes to him. However, now they all knew he had killed Jack MacAdams. They had to die in a way that could be easily understood. He could kill them all right now, because he figured he could make it back to his Tahoe without leaving any telltale evidence for crime scene investigators, even if someone called 9-1-1 as soon as they heard shots and a response team was dispatched immediately.

Dee's voice quivered with fear as spoke. "I should have come forward years ago," he said. "I knew you killed Coach Mac. I saw you come back to the campsite after Jessica left. He was holding the back of his head, standing near the edge of the cliff when you sneaked up behind him. But when the rain started falling and the thunder rolled and lightning flashed in the sky, he turned and saw you coming at him."

"*She* told me the bastard was gay!" Craddock pointed the pistol directly at Jessica. "I had to find out for myself, so I asked him point blank. He admitted he was gay and said it was none of my business."

"And?"

"And he shoved me away. Called me a worthless punk."

"So you decked him … a drunk and critically injured man … and he fought back … and *you*, in what I can only describe as a fit of rage, wrestled him to the ground and smashed his head with a rock. Not once, but three times! Then you carried his body on your shoulders and dumped him over the canyon wall. And I saw it all."

Rhett glared at Dee with a hint of satisfaction. "Right. And then I covered all my tracks, threw the rock over the cliff, and the rain did the rest."

As she listened to the account of what had happened, Jessica's emotions boiled over. "You rotten son-of-a-bitch!" Desperately, she reached into her handbag for the gun.

Craddock saw it coming. In an instant he fired two shots. The first pierced Jessica's heart; the second shattered her cheekbone as she flailed backward from the force of the deadly 9mm bullets.

Blood splattered on Dee's face, and he felt the warm blood running down his neck. He froze and stared at Rhett in disbelief.

"Get over there," Rhett commanded. He pointed the Glock at Lance, who had leaped to his feet when Jessica was shot.

In a matter of seconds, Dee and Lance stood side by side by the coffee table.

With the gun trained on the two men, Rhett kneeled down and pulled Jessica's purse from her grip. He reached inside and found her

.22 Magnum. "You know, Dee, she was coming to kill you because she thought *she* killed Jack MacAdams. And if you had *his* ring, then you must have seen her do it. So *this* is *your* gun." Rhett held the Glock by the silencer and held it out for Dee to take.

Both Dee and Lance noticed the surgical rubber gloves he was wearing on both hands.

Dee shook his head, refusing to take the gun.

"Don't worry. It's empty now. There were only two rounds in the magazine. Now take it! Or I'll blow your head off with *this*!" Rhett straightened his arm and pointed Jessica's Magnum a few feet from Dee's face. His words seeped through clenched teeth and he appeared to become more agitated as he spoke. "So you're another one of those gay *caballeros*, huh?" he said, the contempt dripping from each word. "Now take it!"

Reluctantly, Dee took the gun by the handle knowing his fingerprints would be the only ones there. If Rhett's story was correct, there were no bullets in the chamber, so it was of no use to him. Only Rhett.

"Where did it all go wrong, old buddy?" Lance asked, trying to delay the inevitable.

Rhett continued to point the Magnum at Lance and Dee. "Nothing went wrong, Sir Lancelot. MacAdams was a faggot. You knew that. I always wondered if you were one, too. Especially when I heard what he did to you in the training room. And your faggot friend, here? His so-called coming out didn't surprise me at all. Now both of you get over there!"

With the gun pointing directly at Dee's face, Rhett pointed to the fireplace, where he had been standing when he shot Jessica.

As the two men moved toward the fireplace, Rhett stepped behind Jessica's body, taking care not to touch the blood splotches on the Oriental rug. "Now point that gun at me, Dee," Rhett said with a smile on his face. "And pull the trigger." He began to chuckle loud enough for them to hear, pleased with himself for the way he had created the scenario on the fly. "You had every right to kill her. She came here to kill you with *this*. It's just too bad Sir Lancelot got caught in the crossfire."

Lance knew his old teammate was about to blow. He had to act now.

Rhett straightened his arm and aimed the Magnum at Dee's chest. "Now pull the trigger, you faggot!"

With his eyes glued on Rhett's, Lance could see Jeffrey in his peripheral vision, standing behind Rhett and holding a pistol with both hands, trembling. Even from a distance, Lance could discern the barrel of the gun shaking.

"Fire!" Lance screamed as he slammed his shoulder into Dee's torso.

Three shots rang out.

Lance felt the hot sting of a bullet ripping through his back, the momentum from his blow to Dee's chest spinning both of them to the floor.

Rhett's second shot ricocheted off the white brick fireplace and shattered the picture window behind the dining room table.

Jeffrey shook uncontrollably as he watched Rhett twist to the floor in anguish.

The Magnum clanked on the hardwood floor, and Craddock struggled to unstrap the department-issued .357 in his holster.

With the pistol shaking in both hands, Jeffrey stepped cautiously toward Craddock, pointing the gun at him, ready to fire again. He stopped ten feet from him, the gun still aimed at his head.

Outside, the first responder from the Boulder Police Department, a relatively junior sergeant on Watch Three, quickly assessed the situation from the front deck of the house. He had a clear view of Jeffrey standing over a man on the floor, brandishing his weapon; he could see Dee sitting with his back lodged against the fireplace, a body draped over his outstretched legs.

"I need backup out here immediately," the officer whispered huskily into his headset radio. "There are at least two persons down. Gun in sight. I'm going in now!"

Before the dispatcher could respond, the officer smashed the heel of his boot against the lock securing the double doors leading from the front deck into the family room. His quick analysis of the lock and door frame proved to be correct. With a loud whomp, the door flew open and he burst into the room with his .357 handgun aimed at Jeffrey. "Drop it!" the sergeant yelled, his knees bent and both arms parallel to the floor.

Slowly Jeffrey raised both arms above his head and shouted, "I called 9-1-1!"

Within a minute, two additional squad cars arrived with lights flashing and sirens blaring. One of the officers took the gun from Jeffrey's hand while the other cleared each room.

"My friend's been shot! Please help him," Dee cried, pointing to Lance, whose limp body pinned him to the floor. An officer rushed to his side.

The sergeant knelt next to Jessica and touched her throat with his fingertips. "She's dead," he said solemnly. He turned his attention to the man lying in a pool of blood beside her. He checked for vitals and carefully rolled him over. When he saw the man's face, he said in disbelief, "Chief Craddock?"

Rhett opened his eyes momentarily and slumped in his officer's arms.

The sergeant immediately keyed his radio and said, "We have one dead and two down with gunshot wounds. We need paramedics and ambulance on Knollwood ASAP!" Instinctively, he checked his watch to see how long it would take for medical assistance to arrive, for often it meant the difference between life and death. *11:43 p.m.* "And you better notify Chief Quincy. We have an officer-involved shooting out here."

Six minutes later the paramedics showed up. It took only three minutes to load Chief Craddock and Lance Carpenter into two separate ambulances, and four and a half minutes later they pulled into the emergency room entrance at Boulder Community Hospital.

By the time Chief Quincy arrived on the scene, the three police officers had taken statements from Dee and Jeffrey. The detective on call and a detective sergeant were dispatched to the hospital to provide police security for Chief Craddock and Lance Carpenter. They would determine the next steps in the investigation and when and where the initial interviews of these material witnesses would take place.

Chief Quincy listened carefully to the sergeant's report while Dee and one officer waited in the family room. Jeffrey and the third officer sat downstairs in Jeffrey's living area. A photographer had taken pictures of the scene; Jessica's body had been placed in a body bag, loaded onto a stretcher, and carried down the staircase to a third ambulance waiting for its cargo in front of the garage with rear doors open. Unceremoniously, the medics carrying the stretcher pushed it into place and strapped it down, and within a matter of minutes were bound for the county morgue.

When he had heard enough, Chief Quincy said, "Okay, Mike. Good job. This is going to get some media attention, so let's make sure we've done everything right and get all the facts to our public information officer. She'll handle all the press inquiries."

"Yes, sir. We'll secure the scene and leave a liaison officer here until further notice."

"Very good. What else do we need to think about?"

The sergeant thought for a moment. "What about Chief Craddock?"

"What do you mean what about Chief Craddock? You took the statements. But until he's had a chance to tell his side of the story, we shouldn't speculate or comment during an ongoing investigation. Right?"

"Right, sir."

The Chief smiled and said, "Now you're in charge here, Mike. I'm going back to bed."

"I've got it, Chief," he replied with confidence.

Within an hour, Boulder detectives arrived to begin collecting evidence. They relieved the first responders, who resumed their patrol of the city. Before the liaison officer left the scene, he cleared Dee and Jeffrey to make phone calls.

Jeffrey declined, and after Dee's consoling and reassuring, he returned downstairs to his living area.

Dee immediately called Kimberly Carpenter.

CHAPTER TWENTY EIGHT

～

A couple of minutes short of one o'clock in the morning, the telephone rang in the Carpenter's suite at the St. Julien Hotel. Lance had left for Dee's home a couple of hours ago, and Kimberly had fallen asleep with the television on. She cracked her eyes open when she heard the sound, and she watched the red light illuminate with each ring.

Expecting the call to be from Lance, she shuffled her body over to his side of the bed and reached for the telephone on the nightstand. Then she laid her head back on his pillow and said, "Hello, dear."

"Kimberly, this is Dee," the strange voice said.

"Dee?"

"Yes, it's me. Lance was here and something terrible has happened. Now don't panic. He's going to be okay, Kimberly, but he's been shot."

For a moment, there was dead silence, and then she blurted out, "What? He's been shot!"

Kimberly sat straight up and swung her feet to the floor. She stood beside the bed staring at the wall.

"They're taking him to the emergency room at Boulder Community Hospital. I'm going there to see him."

"Shot?" she asked again, her voice signaling an escalation of anxiety.

"The paramedic said he's going to be okay, Kimberly," Dee reassured her. "I'll tell you what happened when I see you. I'm leaving now, and I'll be at the hotel in less than five minutes. Meet me out front."

"Okay." She heard the click of a terminated call. "Oh, my God," she said, still holding the telephone to her ear. "He's been … *shot!*"

When Kimberly tried to replace the receiver back on the telephone, she realized her hands were shaking. *How in the world could he have been shot?* Her mind flashed as she slipped out of her night shirt and quickly dressed in the clothes she had laid out for the flight back to Boston.

She noted the time: *1:01 a.m.* Knowing Dee would be at the hotel soon, and desperate to see her husband, Kimberly made a quick check in the bathroom mirror and then hurried to meet Dee at the front entrance to the hotel.

As she passed through the lobby, she heard boisterous laughter and the gaiety of a Saturday night. A number of people she had seen at the dinner dance had gathered for a nightcap at the T-Zero hotel bar. They had spilled out of the bar, commandeered tables and chairs in the spacious lobby, and rearranged them for a continuation of their partying.

One of them recognized Kimberly Carpenter when she walked by their group. "Hey, where's the old QB?" he yelled at her. "You guys want to join us?"

Kimberly pretended not to hear and ignored the questions. She stopped by the front door where she could see the entrance courtyard. A minute later she felt a gentle tap on her shoulder. She turned to see who it was, but she did not recognize the man towering above her.

"Pardon my rudeness, Mrs. Carpenter," he said politely. "I'm Larry Tate. I was one of your husband's wide receivers. A bunch of us football players are over there, and we were just wondering if you'd like to join us for a nightcap. We didn't get to see much of you at the dinner dance."

"Lance isn't here," she said anxiously, turning her head to see if Dee had arrived. "He had a meeting with Dee Evans …" she paused, wondering whether she should say anything more.

Tate's mind whirled when he heard Dee's name. Then he saw his car turn into the entrance court and stop abruptly. In a flash, Dee came through the doors to find Kimberly. He was surprised to see Larry Tate standing beside her.

"Let's go," Dee said, taking Kimberly by the arm.

"What's going on here?" Tate asked.

"It's Lance. He's been shot," Dee replied. "We're going to the hospital to see him."

Larry Tate was dumbfounded. He stood speechless by the front door as he watched Dee and Kimberly get into the car and speed away. Then he returned to the table where his old teammates were laughing, carrying on and having a good time.

"Guess what? Lance Carpenter's been shot!"

* * *

Boulder Community Hospital was less than a mile from the St. Julien. Dee sped east on Walnut a short distance, turned left on Broadway and headed straight to the hospital's emergency room on Balsam.

Because traffic was light after midnight, it took less than two minutes to get to the hospital. He had focused all of his attention on getting there safely, and he did not want to begin telling her what had happened. Similarly, she had been numbed by worry and her only concern was for Lance, so she simply sat and stared out the front windshield as Dee raced to the hospital and whipped into an empty space in the parking lot.

A minute later, Dee and Kimberly stood at a counter in the ER where a receptionist wearing light green scrubs talked to two Boulder police officers. They were not the same ones who had responded to the 9-1-1 call at Dee's home.

Dee overheard parts of the conversation, and he knew they were talking about their Deputy Police Chief. He turned his back to the uniformed officers and spoke quietly to Kimberly, his first words since they had left the hotel. Dee leaned closer to her and whispered, "Rhett Craddock shot him. He tried to kill me."

"What?"

"Craddock shot Lance. I'll bet those cops are here to see him."

Kimberly looked over Dee's shoulder. She had not noticed the officers when she and Dee entered the emergency room. "Rhett Craddock tried to kill you?" she asked incredulously.

"Yes, he came to my house to kill me because I knew he killed Jack MacAdams thirty years ago. He didn't know Lance was going to be there."

"I've got to sit down," Kimberly said, suddenly feeling lightheaded and overwhelmed.

Dee wrapped an arm around her waist, and together they sat down in two chairs along the wall.

"Are you okay?" he asked.

"Rhett Craddock killed the coach, and he tried to kill you?"

Dee nodded and said, "Lance saved my life, Kimberly. He shoved me aside just as Craddock fired his gun, and he got hit instead. He literally saved my life, took a bullet for me."

"Oh, my God! Is he okay?"

"I think so. He was conscious when they put him in the ambulance, and the last thing he said to me was, 'I told you I should never return to Colorado.'"

"I've got to see him, Dee."

"I'll let them know you're here."

When Dee returned to the check-in counter, the cops were gone. He waited while the receptionist wrote on a form on a clipboard, and as she finished, he said, "Lance Carpenter, a gunshot wound. That's his wife over there. Can we see him?"

She picked up another clipboard, reviewed the entries and replied, "No, not yet. A doctor will give you a full report as soon as he can. The waiting room is down the hallway to your left."

"What can I tell Mrs. Carpenter?"

The receptionist glanced again at the clipboard, and with an ominous tone said, "I'll ask an attending to talk with her."

"Is he going to be okay?" Dee pressed for any information he could get, knowing they'd have to wait for word from the ER physicians.

"The attending will answer all your questions, sir."

"Okay, thank you. I understand." Dee turned away to go back with Kimberly, and then he stopped. "One more thing," he said to the receptionist. "Has Chief Craddock been admitted tonight?"

Her penetrating eyes answered the question first, and without referring to any paperwork she said, "I'm sorry, sir. I can't give out information on any other patients."

"We'll be in the waiting room," Dee said with disappointment.

After a short walk, Dee and Kimberly found two comfortable chairs in a corner of the waiting room. Magazines and an empty Coke can on the table between them gave an impression of untidiness. The recessed incandescent lighting in the room provided a stark and sterile setting; a row of vending machines provided a selection of drinks and snacks.

Along a windowless wall, an elderly woman sat alone, her fingers knitting furiously, a ball of pink yarn dancing in her lap.

In the opposite corner, a young couple occupied a loveseat, him with his head laid back and his mouth wide open, and her stretched out with her head on his lap. Both slept while they waited.

"It might be awhile, Kimberly. We have to wait for someone to give us a report."

She heaved a sigh and said, "I can't just sit here and wait, for heaven's sake. My husband's been shot and he's in the emergency room. We don't know how bad it is ... how long he'll be in there ... when we can see him. Can't we do *something*?"

"We just have to wait to hear."

A few minutes later, a young woman in scrubs came into the waiting room and said, "Mrs. Carpenter?"

Dee raised his hand. "Over here."

The doctor dragged the nearest straight-backed chair over to where Dee and Kimberly were sitting. She sat down and folded her hands in her lap.

Kimberly saw the blood stains on her shirt. "How is he?"

The doctor leaned forward and gently touched Kimberly's knee. "He has a very serious gunshot wound, but we do not believe it is life threatening. We've stopped the bleeding, got him stabilized. The bullet's still in there, so we have to take him to X-ray to see exactly where it is. Then we'll know exactly what we have to do. I think, maybe … two hours … you'll be able to see him."

"Two hours?"

"It's a very serious wound, Mrs. Carpenter, but we'll be taking good care of him. I promise you that." The doctor patted Kimberly's knee before she stood up and hurried back to the emergency room.

Dee and Kimberly felt a ray of hope, but they still had many questions.

*   *   *

The doctor was wrong. It was not two hours. It was four. Dee and Kimberly were emotionally exhausted by the time the doctor finally came to give them all the details of Lance's condition. The clock on the wall showed *5:39 a.m.*

The X-rays confirmed Craddock's .22-mm bullet had entered Lance's back below the left shoulder, shattering his scapula and lodging dangerously close to the chest cavity. If it had been an inch or two closer to the center of his body, the bullet would have collapsed the lung and most likely exited through his chest, unless it hit a rib.

The ER team had consulted with an orthopedic doctor and a plastic surgeon, and they had decided to leave the bullet right where it was. There would be no negative consequences, except for getting through screening at airport security. The scar on his back would be proof of Lance's heroics for the rest of his life.

After listening intently to the doctor's report, Kimberly asked, "Can we see him now?"

"Yes, come with me. He's sleeping, but you can see him."

They followed the doctor into the ER. She led them to a cubicle created by curtains hung from aluminum tubes attached to the ceiling. Through the curtain separating patients, they heard a child crying while a nurse explained to the parents why surgery was necessary.

Kimberly stood beside the bed in the dimly lit space. A light blanket covered his chest; an IV needle was taped to his right arm; a bundle of colored wires leading to a bedside monitor provided constant readouts of his blood pressure, heart rate and oxygen saturation.

She gazed down at her husband's face, suntanned and healthy, with no obvious indication of the trauma he had been through over the past six hours. She looked at him as he slept and wanted to bend down to hold him, knowing full well she should not. She felt helpless, a sense of deep sorrow, and she began to cry. Then she turned away and walked straight to Dee's open arms.

He held her for a moment and then offered, "I'll stay here with you, Kimberly."

"You don't have to."

"I know, but I want to finish telling you what happened and how Lance and Jeffrey saved my life."

With Lance sleeping peacefully, Dee pulled two chairs to Lance's bedside, and he and Kimberly spoke quietly while they waited for him to awaken. He told Kimberly everything—that Jessica had showed up while he and Lance were meeting, that Craddock had shot her in cold blood because she knew that he had killed Jack MacAdams. He explained how Jeffrey was troubled when Jessica came to the door, and rather than going to bed as he said he'd do, he climbed the stairs and listened to the confrontation. He heard the whole confession and knew Craddock was going to kill everyone in the house.

"So he goes downstairs, gets a gun from my cabinet behind the bar, and comes back upstairs just as Craddock shoots Jessica. Lance and I are going to be next, but Jeffrey sneaks into the room. Lance sees him and yells 'Fire!' Jeffrey fires his gun a split second before Rhett fired at me."

Kimberly was transfixed by every word she heard, then she heard her husband's voice.

"And he shot me instead," he said weakly.

Kimberly stood and turned her attention to her husband.

Lance smiled at her. "It's sure nice to see friendly faces."

She leaned forward and held his hand while they kissed. "How're you feeling?" she asked when their lips parted.

"Better, now that you're here," he answered, still managing to smile. "How long have I been in this place?"

"About five hours. It's almost six o'clock in the morning," Dee chimed in.

"That means it's eight o'clock in Boston. Have you called the girls and JP to let them know what happened, and that I'm going to be just fine?"

"No. Not yet. We've been right here the whole time, waiting to see you. We got the doctor's report only a few minutes ago, but we still don't know how long they're going to keep you here."

"They told me I'd be released before noon, and that I can fly back home today. All we have to do is let JP and the pilots know they're med-evacing a patient with a bullet in his shoulder blade, and if they approve we'll be back in Boston tonight."

Kimberly questioned the wisdom of flying back so soon. "Are you sure you're okay to travel?"

"They said if I have someone to take care of me, it's okay. You'll be right there with me, won't you?"

Kimberly bent down to answer with a gentle hug.

When he tried to lift his arms to hug her back, he cried out in pain, and with his smile replaced by a grimace, Lance said resignedly, "Let's wait to see how I feel after a few more hours of sleep. Better call JP and the girls and let them know what happened."

Then he closed his eyes, and soon thereafter, he slept peacefully again. Kimberly stayed by his side while Dee informed JP Tompkins of Lance's wound, and another death in Colorado.

CHAPTER TWENTY NINE

≈

"Absolutely not," JP Tompkins thundered. "He stays there 'till I get there. I don't care if the doctors said he can fly or not. I don't want him moved until he's fully recovered. I'm going to call my pilots and see how soon we can take off."

"I'll let Lance and Kimberly know," Dee said, sensing JP's urgency.

"I want to see you, too."

Dee thought before responding. "I'll cancel my flight to San Jose this morning. I'd like to meet you in person."

"That's what I have in mind. If you haven't signed the contract, then I'll sign it myself. And we'll sign it in my Denver office tomorrow, with everyone present for the occasion. Now I need to get moving, so thanks for the call."

When Dee returned to the ER, Lance was sitting up in bed talking with Kimberly, who stood by his side holding his hand. "He's awake," he said to Kimberly. Addressing Lance, he asked, "How you doing, old buddy?"

"Doing okay, except for a bullet in my back."

"They've got him on Demerol," Kimberly added. "But he's still feeling some pain. Aren't you, dear?"

"Not so much that I can't get out of here."

"I just talked to JP," Dee said, his twinkle telegraphing another surprise. "He's coming here today, and we're signing the contract in Denver tomorrow."

"You gotta be kidding me."

"Nope. He's scrambling a couple of pilots and flying another one of his jets out here. They should be arriving this afternoon, he said. He also said he's tired of you screwing things up, and he's going to take care of business himself."

Lance frowned as he searched for a more comfortable position on the bed. "Really?"

"No. Not really." Dee grinned with satisfaction, knowing he had injected a little humor into the situation.

Lance managed a smile. Then he chuckled, his shoulders moving with each laugh. "Ahhh!" he cried out suddenly.

Immediately Kimberly began tending to him while Dee's grin turned to a concerned stare.

"What is it, dear?" she asked.

"It's the pain," he answered, his face contorted in anguish.

"Where?"

Lance slowly raised his right arm and pointed an index finger directly at Dee. "Right over there!" he said triumphantly, knowing he had returned the lighthearted favor.

"You must be feeling okay. You haven't lost your sense of humor."

"Lose that and you're dead meat."

"You know, dear, if they said you could be released by noon, and if you're really feeling okay, we could go back to the hotel and let them know we'll be staying another night or two."

"I don't think how I'm feeling has anything to do with it. They're not going to keep me in the ER. And I don't need to convalesce in some hospital room. I need to get to a nice comfortable bed and get some sleep."

Dee listened to their thoughts and then offered, "How about this— call me when you're released and I'll take you back to the hotel. JP's going to call when his flight is confirmed, and I'll be meeting him at

Denver International Airport or the Rocky Mountain Regional Airport, wherever they land. Depending upon what time they arrive and where he plans to stay, he'll see you either tonight or tomorrow morning before the signing in the Denver office."

"Sounds like too many variables to me. How 'bout we just get me back to the St. Julien where I can sleep without all these wires and needles sticking in me. Kim can be my nurse. Can't you, sweetheart?"

"It will be my pleasure to take care of you."

"Very well, then I'll leave you two alone. You've got my cell number, don't you?" Dee questioned.

"It's in my Blackberry," Lance affirmed.

"Good. Then you take care and give me a call when you're ready to go back to the hotel. I'm only five minutes away."

"Will do, and thanks, my friend."

Dee stepped closer to the bed and placed his hand on Lance's shoulder. "No. Thank *you*. Thank you for saving my life—*again*!"

"Isn't that what friends are for?" Lance said emphatically, not asking a question, but making a statement.

Dee simply smiled and gently squeezed Lance's shoulder.

"Ouchhh," he moaned, drawing out the word.

"Did that hurt?"

Lance nodded meekly.

"Really?" Dee wondered.

"No. *Not* really," Lance said with an I-gotcha-grin.

Dee laughed and said, "Call me when you need a lift to the hotel." He opened the curtain and was surprised to see the two policemen he had seen earlier at the ER welcome counter. They were standing outside Lance's cubicle, apparently waiting for Dee.

One of them said, "Mr. Evans, you'll have to come with us. The detectives have a few more questions for you."

"Why's that? I've already told them everything I know."

"Please, come with us," the other one insisted.

"Am I under arrest?" Dee wanted to know.

"No, sir, we just have some additional questions for you. It should not take very long."

Reluctantly, Dee accompanied the policemen as they left the ER, put Dee in the back seat of the cruiser and headed for the Boulder Police Department.

The Carpenters had heard the conversation through the curtain. They were alone, but with fabric-thin walls in the ER cubicles, they talked quietly about what had happened at Dee's house. They speculated about why he had been summoned for additional questioning, and they wondered if he would be able to take them back to the St. Julien as promised.

They also talked about JP's plans for an unscheduled flight to Colorado. If he really wanted to sign the contract in the Denver office with everyone present, then he had another purpose in mind.

Lance and Kimberly Carpenter refused to speculate about JP's full intentions. Rather, for once in their life, they focused entirely on their own selfish priorities—a man with a bullet in his back and a few hours of uninterrupted sleep.

CHAPTER THIRTY

~

Within two hours of receiving the call from JP Tompkins, the chief pilot and a second pilot had the first company Gulfstream 200 rolling down the runway at Logan International Airport bound for the Rocky Mountain Metropolitan Airport in Colorado. For the past year, JP had flown only on his personal jet, but it was already in Colorado, waiting for Lance and Kimberly Carpenter's return flight to Boston. However, with Lance the victim of a shooting and with the lucrative contract with Dee Evans unsettled, JP decided he needed to be there in person as soon as possible.

He had people to make all the arrangements. The pilots took care of the aircraft and the flight planning; his chief of staff booked a two night stay at the Westin-Westminster Hotel for both him and Marcella Rhodes, who, on the same short notice he had given every one else had agreed to be at Logan at eleven o'clock on a Sunday morning for an emergency meeting in Colorado the next day.

With headwinds making the flight a few minutes longer than planned, the transportation arranged by the Denver office had been in place for less than five minutes when the Gulfstream 200 parked on the ramp at the Denver Air Center.

From JP's perspective, everything was moving like clockwork.

However, from the perspective of the interim VP assigned to run the Denver office following Christine Duncan's suicide, responding

176

to the CEO's unscheduled visit to Colorado was total chaos. He was visibly rattled from the time he got the call from JP Tompkins himself to the time he met the corporate Gulfstream on the ramp. He was also relieved when JP opted for little conversation, jumped in the backseat of a limo and hurried off to the hotel in Westminster. By the time he got home to a wife and three children disappointed by his breach of promise to take them to the Butterfly Pavilion, he wanted a stiff drink of scotch on the rocks.

Though they had been on the airplane together for more than four hours, JP had communicated very little with Marcella. He told her what had happened over the past few days: Lance had informed Christine of impending changes; Christine committed suicide; Lance got shot last night; the contract with Evans Software Solutions is up in the air; he has to make some immediate changes in leadership—little things like that.

Marcella figured that if she was along with the CEO to address "little things like that," then she must be in "pretty good shape."

JP gave absolutely no indication of what he had in mind, so she did what any up-and-coming senior executive would do—she did whatever the Chairman asked her to do, and she did it with a smile on her face.

Her next assignment would be to accompany him to the Denver office of Diversified Global Investment Bank for a meeting with all employees at nine o'clock in the morning. They'd be leaving the hotel at 8:30 a.m. sharp.

* * *

When Dee was taken to the Boulder Police Department, he could not have known he would be unable to assist JP with transportation and lodging arrangements as he has offered to do.

As good fortune would have it, his help was not necessary, because JP acted independently of everyone. *He* was the decision maker, and everyone within his organization knew that. He had tasked his people with deciding where he would stay and how he would get there, and with having everyone in the Denver office present at nine o'clock in the morning. That included Dee Evans and Lance Carpenter, assuming he would be medically cleared for travel by then. JP would take it from there.

Dee waited patiently in a police holding room along with an inebriated, scruffy forty-something man wearing faded jeans and no shirt, a pair of worn flip-flops and colorful tattoos on both arms. He carried on about police brutality and insisted that he had been inappropriately taken from the street corner where he was protecting a solitary traffic light from attack by stray dogs running rampant in the neighborhood. Why the police incarcerated him instead of ridding the neighborhood of these vile creatures was beyond his comprehension. In his drunken state, of course, everything was beyond his comprehension.

Finally, Dee was ushered in to a small interrogation room on the ground floor. There were two chairs, one on each side of a table large enough to separate the interrogator from the detainee, and small enough for every word of the interview to be heard. Visible on the wall behind the interrogator was a yellow tape measure used as a backdrop for official photographs. Not visible were the microphones and video camera that recorded every minute of the conversation. Because the investigation centered on an officer-involved homicide, the department's chief detective conducted the interview.

"Here's what we have so far," the detective began, referring to a yellow notepad as he talked. "Deputy Chief Rhett Craddock has been critically wounded and remains in intensive care. A man who says he lives at your home, a Jeffrey Dietz, has been taken into custody and is being questioned for his involvement in the shooting. A second victim, Lance Carpenter, is at the Boulder Community Hospital recovering from a gunshot wound in the back. And a third victim, Jessica Malone, was pronounced dead on the floor in your living room. An investigation is ongoing, and your statement will be part of the investigation. Now, is what I've said so far accurate?"

"It's basically true, except we were in the family room, not the living room."

"Okay, *family* room." The detective scribbled on his notepad and then asked quizzically, "Lance Carpenter? Wasn't he the quarterback at Boulder High a few years back?"

"Thirty to be exact."

That long ago, the detective mulled for a moment, and then continued his questioning. "And Rhett Craddock was one of his receivers?"

"That's right."

"What were they doing in your house last night?"

"I asked Lance to come over. We had some contracts to sign. The others were not invited."

"So why were they there?"

Dee folded his hands on top of the table. "Before we go any further, do I need an attorney?"

"Not unless you want one. You're not under arrest. We just want to know everything that happened. You can take as long as you'd like."

For the next ten minutes, Dee told what had happened from his point of view, including the details of what he heard Jessica say, what he heard Rhett Craddock say, and how he saw the shooting play out.

Both the detective and the sergeant took notes.

When Dee finished his statement, he sat back and waited for additional questions.

"Is that all?" asked the detective.

"I've told you everything," answered Dee.

"So let me be clear about this," the detective said, his eyes fixed on Dee's. "You said you saw Rhett Craddock kill Jack MacAdams on a camping trip in Eldorado Canyon in 1978—and you did not report that fact until now?"

"That's correct," Dee admitted.

"Were you ever questioned by the police regarding the alleged murder?"

"No. No one ever knew I was there, so there was no reason to question me."

"I see." The detective puzzled for a moment, scribbled on the notepad. "But when the death was ruled accidental by the coroner, you knew better. Right?"

"Right. I knew it was not accidental, and MacAdams did not commit suicide."

The detective was about to ask another question when Dee's cell phone rang.

"Can I take this call?"

The detective nodded.

Dee knew it would be Kimberly Carpenter. He listened for a moment and then said, "I'm at the Boulder PD. You better call JP and let him know I can't meet him at the airport. How's Lance doing?"

The detective circled his index finger in the air a few times signaling for Dee to wrap up the telephone call.

A minute later Dee said, "That's good news. I hope to see you tomorrow, but I don't know what else they have in mind for me here. We'll have to see. You guys get some rest." Dee folded his cell phone, slipped it back into a pocket and turned his attention back to the detective.

"You're very fortunate, Mr Evans. You are not guilty of any crime for withholding information, or obstructing justice relative to the 1978 murder. Even if you had been questioned at the time, the statute of limitations would apply in this case. So, you're free to go. If we need to talk with you again for any reason, we'll give you a call."

"Okay. You have my numbers."

After the interview, the detective escorted Dee to the front entrance of the building. When they passed through the holding room, the drunk was gone and the room was empty, which was not surprising for a Sunday morning in Boulder.

CHAPTER THIRTY ONE

～

The small conference room in the Denver office – the same one Lance Carpenter had used last Thursday to inform staff of impending leadership changes – overflowed with people, including Kimberly Carpenter, Marcella Rhodes and the interim vice president, who all occupied front row seats. Everyone anxiously awaited the arrival of the man himself, Chairman of the Board J. Paul Tompkins, the founder of Diversified Global Investment Bank. They knew something big was going to happen, but no one in the room dared to make a prediction because they knew JP was totally unpredictable.

At exactly nine o'clock, Lance Carpenter walked into the conference room and carefully sat down in the empty seat between Kimberly and Marcella.

The conversation in the room hushed.

A moment later, JP strolled into the room, smiling, looking more like a gentle grandfather at a family gathering than a chief executive who had called an unexpected mandatory meeting for all company employees. "Keep your seats," he said when some people started to rise, prompted by the interim VP, the first one standing, with noticeable perspiration on his forehead. JP added emphasis to his point by signaling with his arm out, palm down, in a way that encouraged everyone to take their seats.

Just like Lance Carpenter had done four days earlier, JP stood a few feet from the front row. Some of the folks in the room had seen him on the LCD screen during quarterly board meetings, but only Lance, Kimberly and Marcella had ever seen him in person.

His striking mane of wavy white hair and deep facial creases made him look many years older than his seventy-two years.

"I want to thank everyone here today," he began. "Not only for responding to my knee-jerk request for a mandatory meeting, but for your good work on behalf of our organization. You know, or maybe some of you don't know, I started this company thirty-five years ago. We've grown from an initial cadre of six to a global business with more than five hundred employees and regional offices in Chicago, San Francisco and Denver. Each of you has contributed to our success, I trust, by performing your personal responsibilities to the best of your ability. If you have done that, then I thank you from the very bottom of my heart. If you have not … if you feel unrewarded for your efforts … or if you believe the company has been unfair to you in any way … then I encourage you to speak with your supervisor. If you are not comfortable doing that, then I invite you to speak with me personally while I'm here."

"Now I suppose many of you are wondering *why* I am here, and that's a fair question. It's the first time I've been to the Denver office in several years, and I regret that."

JP unbuttoned his suit coat and continued, carefully searching for words and doing everything he could think of to create a more relaxed setting. Just by looking around the room, he could tell everyone was on edge – the opposite of the atmosphere he wanted. But he had determined what Denver and the entire Diversified organization needed, so he decided to get straight to the point, relaxed setting or not.

"I'm here today to make some announcements that I'm certain will interest you greatly. Now I won't dwell on the tragic circumstances of the past few days," JP said, delicately acknowledging Christine Duncan's suicide, which shocked the Denver office to the core. "Rather I will share with you my vision for the future, and this morning I will announce my appointment of managing director for the Denver office."

The folks in the front row knew it would be one of them, but knowing JP's management history, they preferred not to guess. They had no choice except to wait for the announcement.

"Effective immediately, your new managing director will be ..." The chairman paused and looked down at Lance and Marcella and Donald Larkin, the person he had tapped as the interim VP in Denver. JP brightened and said, "Marcella Rhodes."

Kimberly turned to Lance and whispered, "Did you know?"

He shook his head, his eyes fixed on JP.

Larkin settled back in his seat and breathed a deep sigh of relief. He looked as if the weight of the world had been lifted from his shoulders. Not only was he not ready for a leadership position, he didn't want one, and the events of the last six weeks had made that crystal clear in his mind.

Kimberly leaned forward and turned her head in Marcella's direction, expecting to see signs of satisfaction. Instead she detected a hint of surprise, and her body language suggested reservations with the appointment.

As usual, Marcella's appearance was perfect, from a tailored, pin-striped business suit to her matching Chanel handbag and shoes. She sat erect with her shoulders rolled back, listening intently to JP's words. *Why didn't we talk about this on the airplane?* she wondered.

"Marcella Rhodes, ladies and gentlemen, your new managing director." When he spoke, he stretched his arm in her direction and motioned for her to join him in front of the crowd that began applauding spontaneously.

Marcella stood, and JP offered his hand, not for a handshake but as a gentlemanly gesture for a lady rising to join him. She took his hand, and to her surprise, JP released his grip and wrapped both arms around her in a warm embrace.

The applause continued until they separated and faced the people in the room. JP knew he had made the right choice, and he beamed with pride at his selection; Marcella knew it was a promotion, meant more money, more prestige, and added another title on her already impressive resume. Her only disappointment was that JP had not shared his decision with her, had kept her dangling with anticipation right up until the last moment. However, she had prepared herself for every possible scenario, including the possibility of taking over the Denver office and a move from Massachusetts to Colorado. She just didn't expect it to happen so fast.

JP sensed approval of his announcement from the people in the room, though he did not consider their views relevant to his decision. Yes, many of them thought their new boss would be Lance Carpenter, but the driving concern for every person in the Denver office was not who would be the managing director, but whether the office would close and they'd have to find a new job. That concern had been addressed, and any lingering fears would be erased by JP's next announcement.

"I'm going to ask Marcella to speak in a minute, but before I do that, I'm going to share more good news with you. This weekend we have reached agreement to proceed with an initial public offering for Evans Software Solutions, an account you've been working on for some time now. Completing all the requirements for the initial public offering will be your top priority for the immediate future, and there will be more to do after that," JP said, directing his last comment to Marcella.

"Now, it was my intention to celebrate this occasion with an official signing for all of you here to witness, but unfortunately, a few things happened over the weekend that changed that. I doubt everyone has heard the news so you will hear it directly from me, because it involves two people you know—Dexter Evans and Lance Carpenter. You may not know they were best friends at Boulder High School, and that they had not seen each other for thirty years—until their class reunion this weekend." JP's smile faded as he spoke. "These two men worked out the agreement and intended to sign the documents at Mr. Evans' home on Saturday night. However, someone broke in to the home while they were there ... and tried to kill Mr. Evans with a handgun," he hesitated and looked down at Lance, who realized JP was about to tell all. "Instead, while reacting to the assault, Mr. Carpenter was shot in the back."

A collective, audible reaction filled the room.

Quickly the Chairman added, "Obviously, Lance Carpenter is okay or he wouldn't be with us today. And Dexter Evans would be here, too, but he had to go back to the Boulder Police Department this morning for some additional questioning. So no signing today. Mr. Evans and Ms. Rhodes will get that finished as soon as possible. Right?"

"Yes, sir."

"Good. Now before I let you get back to work, there's one more piece of good news I'd like to share with everyone here in Denver. Mr. Carpenter, would you join us up here?"

Lance glanced at Kimberly, then gingerly rose to his feet, ignoring a bolt of pain from his gunshot wound. Slowly he stepped to the front and stood at JP's left side, facing the rest of the people in the room.

"How are you feeling?" JP asked, the gentle smile back on his face.

"I'm feeling fine, sir," he lied.

"Very good, very good. And have you enjoyed your reunion in Colorado?"

"It was good to see old friends," Lance lied again.

"Good, good," JP's head bobbed with each word. "But you and Mrs. Carpenter are anxious to get back to Boston? Right?"

"I guess you could say that."

"I'm heading back after this meeting."

Lance shuffled on his feet, beginning to feel a bit uncertain and wondering what the Chairman had on his mind.

"And how do you feel about Marcella Rhodes becoming the managing director here, and handling the Evans account from this point on?"

Lance Carpenter felt the heat of a glaring spotlight, which brought him even more discomfort than the bullet in his back. *What in the world's going on here?* he thought, but instead he answered with his true sentiment, "I think Marcella's absolutely the right person for the job."

"So do I."

You've already made that clear.

"Kimberly, would you come up here, too?" JP's smile broadened from cheek to cheek as Kimberly joined the group standing in front of the conference room. "Are you disappointed I did not make your husband the director here in Denver?"

Tactfully, Kimberly replied, "From what I've heard about Marcella Rhodes, she's the right person for the job." She meant what she said, and Marcella acknowledged with a smile of thanks.

"I'm very pleased to hear you all agree with me ... and I trust my final decision for and on behalf of the Diversified Global Investment Bank will be equally well received." JP squared his shoulders and took a deep breath. He surveyed the faces in the room, a sense of pride evident on his own. "I will be stepping down as Chairman of the Board very soon, and Lance Carpenter will be the new chairman effective December thirty-first."

Lance and Kimberly's heads turned simultaneously to each other, the genuine surprise registered on both of their faces. Yes, they had hoped it would someday happen, but never would they have guessed the decision would be made while they were in Colorado.

Again the small conference room was filled with spontaneous applause, an affirmation that everyone in the Denver office was happy with JP's final announcement.

Everyone that is, except Marcella Rhodes. For her, it had inflicted pain to rival the pain in Lance Carpenter's back. It was centered in the pit of her stomach, but as a testament to her strong willpower, she did not let it show on her face.

CHAPTER THIRTY TWO

〜

That afternoon, JP Tompkins sat alone in the cabin of his personal jet. The one hundred knot tailwinds would help get him back to Boston a half hour earlier than planned. He was pleased with his decision to bail out a couple of years early and turn the company over to Lance Carpenter, the guy he had mentored from the day he came to him as a banged up Boston College quarterback.

JP had insisted that Marcella stay in Colorado for at least two weeks; he had encouraged Lance and Kimberly to stay until he was *really* well enough to travel home. Not only that, he thought they should have a couple of days together to enjoy the prospects of becoming the CEO within the next four months. He reasoned they would have plenty of opportunities to enjoy the Gulfstream 200, for it was purchased with company funds and would remain a company capital asset after his departure.

He might even go to the cockpit and take the controls for awhile. Or he might kick back and grab some sleep. Or pour himself a glass of scotch. Maybe more.

Point is, JP Tompkins thoroughly enjoyed flying alone in his private jet, and if this was going to be one of his last flights in *his* personal aircraft, he was damn sure going to enjoy it.

By the time JP landed at Logan, word of the actions he had taken in Colorado had zoomed throughout the Diversified Global Investment

Bank. So had reports of Lance Carpenter being shot while heroically saving a high school classmate, the founder and owner of a new major account that Carpenter himself had negotiated.

After thirty minutes of pleasantries following JP's landmark meeting in Denver, the Carpenters returned to their suite in the St Julien. He and Kimberly had taken JP's advice and decided to remain in Colorado until Thursday, with recovery and relaxation their top priorities. Lance's Blackberry had become active with e-mail traffic, congratulatory text messages and phone calls, most of which he let go to voice mail.

The one call Lance answered was from Dee Evans, who had just left the police department and insisted upon seeing Lance at the hotel. He, too, had heard about JP's announcement during the morning meeting, and he wanted to congratulate Lance in person. He also had made an important decision impacting the future of Evans Software Solutions, something that would be of great interest to the new chairman of Diversified Global Investment Bank's board of directors.

"Dee's on his way over here," Lance said when the call ended. "He says, 'We need to talk.'"

"You need to lie down. I don't think you should be going to meetings and meeting people. You just got out of the emergency room yesterday for crying out loud."

"I'm feeling better, Kim. The Demerol seems to be working—and I'm taking it easy."

"You never take it easy, Lance Carpenter. You're always on the go."

"Look here," he said, slowly raising his left arm above his head, a confident grin on his face. "It's getting better already."

"Don't push it, my dear. You'll pull some stitches and get blood on your shirt. You should just sit down and relax."

"Now listen, I'm going to be okay. I'm not going to do anything stupid, but I'm not going to stop doing everything. That simply isn't going to happen."

Lance's Blackberry rang again, and when he checked the display, it read *Marcella Rhodes.*

Kimberly shook her head, and when she realized Lance was going to take another business call, she left the room, perturbed.

"Lance Carpenter."

"Hello, Lance, this is Marcella. Have you spoken to Dexter Evans in the last few minutes?"

"Yes, he's coming to see me at the hotel. He said he needs to talk with me."

"I just got off the phone with him. He's pulling the plug on the contract for his initial public offering."

"Really? Why?"

"He said you'd know why."

"I don't know why he'd do something like that. He's been jacked around, but my latest understanding is that we're all set to go."

"Right, but he said what happened last night has changed his mind. He said you'd understand."

"Quite frankly, Marcella, I'm baffled, but I guess I'll know more after we've talked. Thanks for the heads up."

"No problem, sir. I just thought you should know."

"Sir?" he questioned immediately. "How about Lance? We've known each other far too long to get formal all of a sudden."

"You're going to be the chief executive officer, and I don't speak with CEO's on a first name basis."

"You better get used to it, Marcella, because when I become the CEO of this company, you'll be one of my top senior executives, and we'll be working on a first name basis. That's what I expect our relationship to be."

"Very well then. *Lance* it will be."

"Thanks, Marcella—and thanks for the heads up. You can call me anytime we need to talk."

"Don't worry, Lance. I will."

* * *

With the temperature a balmy eighty-two degrees at four o'clock in the afternoon, Lance and Kimberly waited for Dee on a patio accessible through the lobby of the St. Julien. They sat at a table near a rotunda that served as a gateway to a manicured grass courtyard suitable for a cocktail reception, wedding ceremony or even a nice play area for kids. They had stopped at the T-Zero bar for two glasses of KJ chardonnay and a bowl of mixed nuts, even though she cautioned him against mixing Demerol with wine.

"There he is," Kimberly said, waving at Dee as he walked through the double glass doors.

Dee marched straight to the table, pulled back one of the leather-strapped chairs and sat down. "I'm sorry I missed the meeting with JP," he said. "The Chief of Police wanted to see me before the press conference this morning. No big deal, but the timing couldn't have been worse."

"Everything okay?"

"Yeah. Craddock's going to survive, but he's looking at murder one."

Kimberly spoke up, "He deserves everything he'll get. What's the punishment for murder in Colorado.?"

"I don't know, but it's probably life in prison or possibly even death. I never thought about it."

"Do you want something to drink?" Lance asked.

Dee stood up and said, "I'll get a Coke. You guys want anything else?"

"We're fine," Lance answered as Dee returned to the hotel in haste. "He seems a little edgy."

"We'll find out why," she said. Kimberly tipped her glass and slowly drew a sip of chardonnay. "My guess is they're investigating both of the murders, making certain they have statements from all the eye witnesses."

"They don't have mine."

"They will ... before you return home."

"You sound like a district attorney."

"It's my training in criminal justice kicking in, but I gave that dream up a long time ago."

A few minutes later, Dee backed through the door and returned to the table carefully snuggling a can of Coke, a glass filled with ice and a basket of popcorn against his chest.

Kimberly saw a potential accident in the making and met him a few feet away. "Here, let me take those," she said, reaching for the glass and the popcorn.

"Oh, thank you, Kimberly. You're a lifesaver," he said overdramatically.

"*He's* the lifesaver around here," she said, deflecting the compliment to her husband.

Lance smiled and swallowed a mouthful of wine.

Kimberly placed the basket in the middle of the table and handed the glass to Dee, who waited for her to sit.

Dee plopped down in the chair and poured Coke over the ice, a crown of bubbles threatening to spill over the rim. He waited and then continued pouring, this time aiming the stream of Coke on the side of the glass rather than over the ice cubes. When the glass was full, he set the can on the table, raised the glass for a toast and said, "Cheers … to the man who saved my life … and to his beautiful lady. I love you guys!"

"Cheers," they echoed together.

After the toast, Lance started the conversation. "I just got a call from Marcella Rhodes. She said you're having second thoughts on the contract."

"Damn, word travels fast. I spoke with her when I was leaving the police department less than twenty minutes ago."

Lance studied Dee's eyes and waited for him to continue.

Dee scooted forward in his chair to set the glass down. His hand was wet from the moisture on the glass, so he grabbed a napkin, crumpled it between his palms for a few seconds and tossed it back on the table.

"I'm not going to go public with my company. I'm going to sell it," Dee declared. "After everything that's happened over the weekend, I've decided to make some major changes in my life."

"Going public with your company will certainly change your life. I guarantee it."

"I know, Lance, but for me, right now, going public with my life is more important than Evans Software, or money, or anything in the whole wide world. You know, the journeys we've all been on for the past thirty years have been pretty remarkable. But I've lived in two completely different worlds—my professional business world and my private social world. I've kept them separate, and that's what's going to change."

Dee leaned toward the table and fumbled for the napkin. He used it to dab tears that had welled up uncontrollably. "When I saw Rhett kill Jessica ... and I saw his gun pointing at me ... the rage in his eyes ... the venom in his words. That's when my life began to change. He wanted to kill me not because I knew he had killed Jack, but because I am gay."

"We would both be dead if it weren't for Jeffrey," Lance interjected.

"I know. I would have been next."

"Then me."

"And then Jeffrey—and I shudder to think what he would have done to him. A bullet through the heart would have been a blessing. I owe a lot to that young man."

Kimberly squirmed in her seat as the events of Saturday night were replayed. "The blessing is the two of you are still alive to talk about it."

"You're right, Kimberly. I owe my life to this man. He was all I had in high school—until I was attracted to Jack MacAdams. He cared for me, too, but in a different way. And when I watched how he died, when I saw Rhett Craddock raise a boulder above his head and smash it down on him ... again and again?" Dee stopped, reliving the savagery of the killing he had witnessed. "It was like every blow buried me deeper and deeper."

Kimberly had inched forward on her seat too, her instinct for justice surfacing again. "Why didn't you report what you saw? There would have been a more thorough investigation, and you wouldn't have had to carry this burden inside for all these years?"

"Good question, Kimberly. That's exactly what the police wanted to know. Like I said, when I saw how brutally Rhett attacked Jack, I was traumatized and my secrets were driven deep into my soul. There was no way I could tell anyone anything. I was terrified ... confused ... just beginning to accept my own sexuality. There's no way a person can understand what it was like, unless that person is gay."

Dee reached for his glass and slid back in his chair, letting his point sink in, doubting that it would. He took another sip of Coke, cradled the glass in both hands, and waited for a response.

"I can only imagine what you've been through during you lifetime," Kimberly said. "Here you are, a successful businessman on the outside, but you must've been dealing with an immense internal conflict that you finally decided to resolve."

"You know, Kimberly, my life has been filled with self doubt, self examination, and an inability to accept myself. Those internal gut feelings led me to meet other gay people, and that allowed me to learn more about sexual orientation. There was conflict in my soul, because I was taught what you were taught—that it's a sin to be gay."

"So you're going to sell Evans Software rather than going forward with an IPO?" Lance asked, shifting the focus of the conversation, sounding a bit more businesslike than he'd intended.

"See there, you're uncomfortable even talking about it."

"No, Dee, your sexuality has nothing to do with what we can do for Evans Software. We can take it public ... we can help you sell it ... we have many investors who will be very interested in whatever you want to do."

"Spoken like a seasoned CEO!"

"Spoken from my heart, Dee. Whatever you want to do, I'm with you. Always have been."

"Always will be?" Dee asked about the unspoken thought.

Lance's hesitation was part of his answer. "I hope so," he said as he reached for his glass of chardonnay and proposed a toast. "To another thirty years!"

All three glasses met above the table, and with the final toast, they were empty.

Lance and Kimberly Carpenter watched Dee Evans disappear through the doors of the St Julien Hotel. With each step, the distance between them became greater and greater. And for all of them, each step in a different direction marked the beginning of a new and exciting phase of their lives.

EPILOGUE

~

For the next two years, Lance Carpenter guided the Diversified Global Investment Bank through the most difficult period in its thirty-seven year history. A meltdown in the financial industry sparked the most severe economic crisis in the country since the Great Depression. Millions of people around the world watched as billions of dollars of wealth were wiped out in a matter of months. The US Government spent $800 billion bailing out Wall Street and the nation's largest banks, and Congress added another $860 billion to fund an economic stimulus package. By the fall of 2009, the national debt was forecast to be $1.4 trillion, triple that of the previous administration. What a time to be in the investment banking business!

But Lance Carpenter met all of the challenges head-on. With the corporation's portfolio decreasing by thirty-four percent and facing dismal projections for at least the next eighteen months, Lance convinced the board of directors to close not one, but two regional offices—San Francisco and Chicago. The Denver office, with Marcella Rhodes doing well as the senior executive, took over all accounts from the San Francisco operation and about half of the Chicago business; the other half absorbed by Boston's staff.

JP Tompkins had been right—Lance Carpenter and Marcella Rhodes were the two rising stars at Diversified Global Investment Bank—and their leadership would be instrumental in positioning the bank for growth when the financial industry rebounded, if and when that happened.

Lance supported and encouraged Kimberly's passion for corporate finance law, where she finally put her JD degree to good use. Her hefty salary as a top attorney turned out to be frosting on top of the Carpenter's total compensation cake.

Even though they were both engaged in separate careers that often demanded their full attention, Lance and Kimberly kept their family ties strong and connected. Their oldest daughter graduated from Boston University in the spring and entered the Harvard Law School three months later, with her excellent scholastic record and her pedigree paving the way. Their youngest daughter decided two attorneys in the family were enough, so she pursued a BS degree in communication with an emphasis in public relations. Her graduation and the weddings of both daughters were the next major milestones for the Carpenter family.

The only disruption in their "new" lives was Rhett Craddock's indictment and trial for two counts of murder in the first degree. The legal proceedings brought two eye witnesses to one of the murders—Lance Carpenter and Dexter Eugene Evans—back together for the second time in the past three decades, this time under significantly different circumstances.

The first time was for their thirty-year high school reunion, an occasion intended to celebrate Dee's selection as the Distinguished Citizen of the Year while Lance conducted business in Colorado. Instead the reunion stoked memories of another murder Dee had witnessed and kept hidden deep inside for the next thirty years.

The second time together for Lance and Dee, the Craddock murder trial, could best be described by one word—closure.

As two individuals who knew both murder victims and their killer as well as anyone, Lance and Dee's testimony detailed events and relationships past and present. Not only did their testimony seal a guilty verdict for Rhett Craddock, the process served to cleanse their individual souls, to rid them of demons they had battled for years.

For Lance Carpenter, he finally rationalized that the sexual abuse inflicted by Father John during his childhood and the incidental encounter with Jack MacAdams during his senior year were regrettable experiences during vulnerable and transformative times of his life, and had nothing to do with his own character or sexuality.

For Dee Evans, the closure was most complete. Craddock had been convicted and was serving a life sentence without parole in the Colorado State Penitentiary. Dee sold Evans Software Solutions for $209 million. For one dollar, he sold his home on Knollwood Drive to Jeffrey, who had become more of a son than a live-in caretaker. Dee moved to a palatial home in Palisades overlooking the Pacific Ocean. As an openly gay philanthropist, he became a vocal gay rights activist and gave millions in support of gay rights and the cause of equal treatment for gay men and women.

With closure comes new perspectives, and perhaps redirection or renewal. Certainly new challenges to be met with refocused energy and purpose. In some cases, it means changing the way one thinks about things, considering different possibilities, reaching for higher goals, hoping for a better world.

Lance Carpenter was deep in thought, sitting alone in the chairman's suite on the thirty-ninth floor of the Prudential Building, when his executive assistant walked into his office.

"Mr. Carpenter?"

"Good morning, Arlene. Is everything ready for the board meeting?"

"Yes, sir. Everything is all set and everyone is in the conference room. Here's your final board book with all the changes you asked for."

"Thanks. Let's go," he said, straightening his maroon and gold tie and heading for the door.

"Sir," she said meekly. "You've got a call on line one."

"What? Are you kidding? The board meeting starts in five minutes."

"I know, but there's someone who insists on talking with you now."

"Oh, come on, you know the rules. I don't take calls before a board meeting."

"It's Dee Evans, sir. He said you'd want to talk with him."

Lance stopped and turned. He smiled and said, "Dee Evans? I haven't talked with him since the trial over a year ago."

"He knows you have a board meeting, but he said he has something important to tell you before the meeting. Won't take long, he said."

That's what he said last time. Lance returned to his desk. "You go on in and I'll take the call. I won't be long."

As Arlene closed the door behind her, Lance picked up the receiver and spoke. "Dee Evans, how the hell are you?"

"Better than the last time we talked."

"Great. It's good to hear your voice, but …"

"I know, you've got a big board meeting, but don't worry, you're the big boss now so you can be a few minutes late."

"Dee …"

"It's okay, this will be a short call. Promise. Rebecca's planning our thirty-fifth reunion and she asked me to ask you if you'd like to be the keynote speaker."

Lance was stunned and speechless for a noticeable span, long enough for his patience to wane and his blood pressure to rise. "You've got to be kidding me. That's three years away!"

Dee guffawed loudly and quickly said, "You're right, Lance, I'm just kidding. It's true Rebecca really is starting to plan the next reunion, if you can believe that. But that's not why I'm calling. I'll be in Boston next month for a gay rights conference, and *I'm* going to be the keynote speaker. I'd like to invite you and Kimberly to be my guests at the dinner."

"You son-of-a-gun, you got me. I hope you're serious about coming to Boston, or I'll really be pissed."

"Yep, I'll be in Boston the weekend of October seventeenth. The dinner is on Friday night."

Lance felt a sense of relief when he heard the date.

He checked his watch. He had two minutes until the start of the board meeting. "I'm sorry, Dee. Kimberly and I won't be here that weekend. We're taking a week off to go to Italy for a few days of real vacation. We're going to Florence, Tuscany, and of course, every good Catholic has to visit Rome. The occasion? We'll be celebrating our twenty-eighth wedding anniversary."

"Congratulations, Lance. You'll really love Italy, especially the small villages in Tuscany. You should check out *Lastra a Signa*, about twenty minutes from Florence. I can recommend a wonderful villa for lodging and a couple of fabulous restaurants if you're interested."

"I am."

"Too bad you'll miss the dinner, and I was also hoping we could go to the BC game on Saturday. By the way, you said you'd call, but my phone hasn't rung."

"We've been real busy, Dee. Kim's working full time and I'm trying to keep this corporation afloat during these unprecedented financial times."

"I know what you mean."

Lance thought for a moment and continued, "Besides, Dee, let's face it. Things are much different between us now."

"Because I bailed on the contract?"

"No, Dee. Not that. We're just—different?"

"Different? You mean I'm gay and you're not."

Lance intentionally waited a few seconds before his answer. "Yes, Dee, because you're gay. I love you as a human being, and I respect what you've done as a businessman, and I understand what you're doing for the gay community."

"But you can't love me as a gay man?"

"Sorry, Dee, I'm not there yet."

For most of the first forty-eight years of his life, Dee had struggled with his own sexual identity and had experienced the wide spectrum of emotions that others showed during relationships with gay persons—

from acceptance to rejection; from love to hate. During the past two years, he had seen how people changed when they found out he was gay, and now his first and best friend was one of them. This time Dee paused before he asked, "Are we still friends?"

"Of course we are," Lance answered with certainty. "I hope to see you at the thirty-fifth reunion."

"That's what I was hoping you'd say. But you know what, Lance, I am who I am. If you had said otherwise, I would have been hurt, but I could accept it."

"Hey, we were best friends for the first half of our lives. No reason we can't stay friends for the second half."

"I like that thought, Lance—and thanks again for saving my life."

"Thanks for the call, Dee. It was good talking with you. You take care."

Lance pressed his finger on the cradle button terminating the call. He punched an open outside line and dialed Kimberly's number at work, hoping she'd pick up.

"Hello, dear," said the upbeat voice on the other end. "To what do I owe the honor of a call at this time of the day? I thought you had a board meeting."

"I do. And I'm late, but I wanted to ask you if you're ready for that vacation you've always wanted."

"Italy?"

"Yes."

"When?"

"Next month. The third week of October."

"Why then?"

"October's the best month to go to Italy?"

"Says who?"

"Says lots of people. Are you up for it or not?"

"I don't know. I'll have to check my busy schedule. When did you get this bright idea?"

"Five minutes ago. We've got an anniversary that week. Remember?"

"Lance Carpenter, I know you. You're not telling me the whole story."

"You're right," he admitted. "Dee Evans just called. He's going to be the keynote dinner speaker at a gay rights convention here in Boston. He invited us to attend."

"When is it?"

"The third week in October"

"We should go to the dinner, Lance. I think it would be a very interesting evening. And besides, don't you think you should be there to support your best friend from high school? I'd like to see him again. Think about it."

"Okay, I'll think about it. We can talk more when I get home. People are waiting for me in the boardroom."

* * *

When Lance walked into the board of directors meeting seven minutes after the published start time, some of the directors gave him a long look. Two of the four video conference screens were dark. In the Denver office, Marcella Rhodes sat at the head of the table drumming her fingers impatiently.

With the demeanor of a seasoned and confident chief executive, Lance took his seat.

"Ladies and gentlemen, good morning," he began. "I'm sorry for being a few minutes late. I got a call from a high school classmate right before the meeting, and we talked longer than expected. His call reminded me of a promise I made twenty-eight years ago, a promise that will require me to be away for a week in October. Mrs. Carpenter and I are going to Italy to celebrate our twenty-eighth wedding anniversary."

A voice to the chairman's right spoke up. "That's the week we play North Carolina State, sir."

"I know. They'll just have to win without us. Now, let's get started with the business at hand." Lance reached for the mahogany gavel and tapped it twice on the table. "First item, annual budget review. Marcella, would you like to go first?"

"Thank you, Mr. Chairman, members of the board, it's a chamber of commerce day in Colorado, and I'm happy to report it's been a very good year for …"

As Marcella began her presentation, Lance wondered if he had done the right thing—and his mind drifted to a distant land. *Italy? I wonder what the weather's like in October.*

Author's Note

~

After my first two historical fiction books were published, an author whose views I highly value recommended that I write a purely fictional story, not based on any persons that I have known or experiences that I have had. Rather, she encouraged me to write about a broken-down plumber in Seattle. Or a woman struggling to go on with her life after the loss of her two-year old son. Or a controversial, socially relevant topic that will incite the emotions of people who read the book.

So I decided to create a story about two men who grew up as best friends in Boulder, Colorado, and because of different interests, went off to college in opposite directions—one to Boston College and the other to Stanford University. Thirty years later they return to Boulder for their thirtieth high school reunion, and when one of the characters declares he is gay, both of their lives are changed forever.

The story contains elements of a mystery with closure for many of the characters. However, the controversial, socially relevant theme embedded in the story—homosexuality and its impact on human emotions—is equally significant.

Writing about this theme as a non-gay person with preconceived notions of my own required me to think deeply about topics like gay rights, gay marriage versus gay unions, our military's "don't ask, don't tell" policy, how gay people are treated in other cultures around the world, and what my Bible has to say about homosexuality.

It was a daunting task for a person with a middle name of Christian; a white, Anglo-Saxon protestant who was raised in middle class America and served thirty-one years in the US Air Force. I must admit that I never gave it much thought until I started writing this book, a process that took approximately two years. During that timeframe the following events occurred:

California's high court allowed gay marriage for six months before voters banned it in November 2008.

On February 19, 2009, the *Chicago Tribune* reported, "A task force of the Evangelical Lutheran Church in America recommended Thursday that its leaders make changes to allow gays and lesbians in committed relationships to serve as clergy."

On April 3, 2009, the Associated Press reported, "Iowa's Supreme Court legalized gay marriage Friday in a unanimous and emphatic decision that makes Iowa the third state—and the first in the nation's heartland—to allow same-sex couples to wed." The same week, Vermont passed a bill legalizing gay marriage over the veto of the Governor.

On May 5, 2009, Maine became the fifth state to approve gay marriage, and six months later, Maine voters followed California's path and repealed the law.

On October 10, 2009, at a dinner in Washington sponsored by the nation's largest gay advocacy group, the Human Rights Campaign, President Barack Obama said, "I will end 'don't ask, don't tell.'" According to reports from dinner attendees, he recounted ongoing efforts to bring full civil rights to gays and lesbians and said, "I'm here with a simple message—I'm here with you in that fight."

On October 28, 2009, when President Obama signed the Matthew Shepard and James Byrd, Jr. Hate Crimes Prevention Act, he reportedly spoke of a nation becoming a place where "we're all free to live and love as we see fit." This legislation, named in part for a gay University of

Wyoming student murdered in 1998, adds crimes based on gender or sexual orientation to the list of federal hate crimes.

In November 2009, the Church of Jesus Christ of Latter-day Saints, which openly campaigned for California's Proposition 8, indicated support for gay rights legislation in Salt Lake City, a position that some critics called a reversal of its position. Mormon officials disagreed, restating the church's belief that homosexuality is a sin and that same-sex marriage poses a threat to traditional marriage.

Each of these events, certainly not an exhaustive list, is indicative of a trend toward more widespread recognition of gay rights in this country. However, some religious groups and individuals view the normalization of gay rights as a threat to the fundamental core values of our society.

In 2008, twenty-nine people were murdered for one reason only—because they were gay. That number represents the highest number of deaths since 1999 and an increase of twenty-eight percent from 2007. In the United States alone, 2,424 injuries were reported, with 216 requiring medical attention, and reports of physical abuse at the hands of law enforcement increased 150-percent, from ten in 2007 to twenty-five in 2008.

In 1993, the US Congress passed "don't ask, don't tell" legislation mandating the discharge of openly gay, lesbian or bisexual service members. More than 13,500 individuals have been discharged under the law since 1994.

A book written thousands of years ago, reportedly the most-read book in history, contains many statements about marriage and homosexuality. The following list provides a few passages for reference:

Leviticus 18:22
Leviticus 20:13
Mark 10:3-10
Ephesians 5:22-23
Romans 1:24-27
I Corinthians 6:9

Rather than quoting scripture, I will summarize my interpretation of the literal message conveyed by these references. For a man to be with another man is an "abomination," and those who commit this abomination will not only be cut off from society, but will be worthy of death.

So will our society become one that condemns an individual who is gay, whether by genetic disposition or personal choice—or accepts the individual as a fellow human being with flaws and feelings, responsibilities and rights?

Should gay marriage be legalized in this country?

Is it right for gay individuals to serve in the military forces that defend our national security?

How do parents accept the fact that one or more of their children are gay, and how are their respective lives changed when this comes out?

Will the forces of evil eventually lead to the destruction of our society as we know it?

Writing this book has not completely answered any of these questions for me. It has simply opened my eyes to a whole new world of important questions that are based not in fiction, but in reality.

I have dedicated this book to "my family and *all* my friends." Two people I count among my friends are representative of the tremendous distance between people with opposing views on homosexuality.

Neil Giuliano, one of my fellow administrators at Arizona State University, remained a deeply closeted gay man until his second term as mayor of Tempe, Arizona. Even though our office doors were side by side, I did not know he was gay, and I was surprised when he came out. From 2005 to 2009, Neil served as President of the Gay and Lesbian Alliance Against Defamation (GLAAD), one of the nation's most active gay rights organizations.

My classmate **Kris Mineau**, a retired Air Force colonel whose distinguished military career spanned the Vietnam conflict and the first Gulf War, has the distinction of surviving a supersonic ejection from his disabled aircraft. Kris currently serves as President of the Massachusetts Family Institute and is one of the country's leading advocates for the institution of marriage and its positive impact on family values.

Both of these friends have shared with me their personal experiences in battling the wide range of human emotions they have experienced during their lives. I respect their individual differences and applaud their efforts to help other people understand their perspectives.

My hope is that this book has stirred your emotions and encouraged you to think about sensitive topics that will be rooted in our world for generations to come. For most of these topics, the divergence of views will remain wide open, and there will be no closure.

Terry Isaacson